OCTOBER OUTLAW

JUSTICE, MONTANA SERIES
- Book Two -

DEBBI MIGIT

Scrivenings
PRESS
Quench your thirst for story.
www.ScriveningsPress.com

Published by Scrivenings Press LLC
15 Lucky Lane
Morrilton, Arkansas 72110
https://ScriveningsPress.com

Printed in the United States of America

Paperback ISBN 978-1-64917-165-8

eBook ISBN 978-1-64917-166-5

Library of Congress Control Number: 2021948008

Editors: Elena Hill and Linda Fulkerson

Cover by www.bookmarketinggraphics.com.

Scripture quotations marked (NIV) are taken from the Holy Bible, New International Version®, NIV®. Copyright © 1973, 1978, 1984, 2011 by Biblica, Inc.™ Used by permission of Zondervan. All rights reserved.

Dedicated to the Flynn family. We are writers, artists, poets, singers, songwriters, crafters of all kinds, photographers, film-makers. Creatives.

A very special thank you to my Flynn cousin, Krista, who helped me thicken the plot.

ACKNOWLEDGMENTS

Keith and Christine, for my peaceful writing retreat. You bless me.

Mom, my best beta reader, who loves everything I write.

Phil, I couldn't do this without your support. Literally. #punsrus

Linda Fulkerson, Elena Hill, and everyone at Scrivenings Press.

Thank you!

1

Sunday, October 7
6:30 p.m.

If I'd known my evening included being stalked by a cougar, I would've worn different shoes. I picture my red Chucks, the right one nestled near my desk, the left one upside down on my overflowing clothes hamper. Now those are cougar-stalking shoes.

I glance at the pointed toes of my black and white cowboy boots. They were a perfect choice to go with my denim skirt and slouchy black sweater when I dressed for church this morning. Wriggling my pinched toes, I jolt as Grace grabs my arm.

"Shh. Quit squirming, Jess, or he'll hear you." Grace's voice trembles, and I don't blame her. At least I have pointy toes to kick my way out of an attack. Grace is wearing ballet flats.

"I wonder if he tracks us by smell?" I ask, regretting I washed my hair this morning with my favorite shampoo, Eden Spring. Then I smile, remembering how much Cole likes my shampoo.

"Are you smiling?" Grace is incredulous. "This is not a smiling situation." She narrows her eyes. "You're thinking about Cole, aren't you?"

My face heats, and I hope Grace doesn't notice in the darkness. "Yes," I admit. "I think he'd be pretty handy right about now, don't you?"

"Especially if he brought Roxie," Grace agrees.

Roxie, Cole's Australian Shepherd, is gentle, but she can be very protective when necessary. Cougar stalking qualifies.

"You know what else would be useful right now?" I add. "A cellphone." I glance at the phone Grace is gripping. "Specifically, one with some battery left."

"Well, at least I brought my phone."

She's right. I forgot my phone. Again. With a weak grin, I suggest, "I suppose you can throw it at the cougar." I make jokes when I'm nervous.

Grace opens her mouth to tell me what she thinks of that plan. But an unearthly scream slices the night, drowning out Grace's soft, Georgia accent, and we echo with our own shrieks.

"He's getting closer. We have to get out of here," Grace states the obvious through chattering teeth.

I peek around the edge of the small utility shed, hoping it conceals us from the largest cougar I've ever seen. I want to kick myself with my pointy-toed boots for insisting we walk this far. Justice, Montana, sits at the foot of the Pioneer Mountains. Usually, the wildlife stays in the mountains, seldom venturing this close to civilization.

I recognized the eerie wail of a cougar a few days ago when Cole and I were leaving our jobs at the Hadley Ranch. But this meeting is my first in person. Or cougar. Or whatever.

Next to me, Grace sniffles, and I squint at her. "Are you crying?"

"No, I'm trying not to sneeze." She scrunches up her nose. We hold our breaths, then sigh as the urge passes. "The Olson's are having a bonfire, and you know what smoke does to my sinuses."

We press against the shed, senses alert for any sign the cougar has found us.

"Ah-choo!"

Grace's blue eyes widen in horror. We both know what's coming next. Grace always sneezes three times. Always.

"Ah-choo, ah-choo." The baby sneezes shake her body but barely make a sound.

A minute passes, then two. Laughter drifts from the Olson's back yard, and I suddenly crave a s'more. And safety. Not necessarily in that order.

Grace touches my hand, and I flinch but continue looking toward the field where we last sighted the cougar. Nothing.

"Jess," Grace murmurs.

"I don't see him. Let's make a break for it." I'm counting on fear and adrenaline to overcome our poor choice of footwear.

Grace squeezes my hand tighter. "Jess."

I give her hand a return squeeze. "We can do this," but I'm interrupted by Grace again.

"Jess!"

Startled, I shift to look at her, but Grace's attention focuses somewhere else. She's staring in stark terror at the massive cougar standing ten yards away. He's eyeing us like we're the main course in an all-you-can-eat buffet. I detect the shimmer of one green eye in the moonlight, and I swear he licks his lips. Knees buckling, I slump against the shed by Grace.

"Grace," I whisper. "Do you notice anything strange about that cougar?"

She looks at me like I've lost my mind.

"You mean other than the fact he wants to devour us?"

"He only has one eye."

"One is all he needs," she says, her tone laced with bitterness.

We each hold our breath as the cat tenses his muscles, preparing to pounce. Then he opens his giant mouth, displaying impressively sharp teeth. Yet instead of another spine-chilling howl, I hear the powerful *whoop, whoop* of a police siren. In a split second, the cougar turns and bounds away, retreating into the timbers where he belongs.

My legs give way, and I join Grace, where she's collapsed to the ground.

Around the corner, men are talking, and I recognize the voice of Deputy Sheriff Nick McBride, Cole's older brother. As a flashlight beam sweeps the pasture, I see Levi Cooper, a Deputy Sheriff Cadet, who has been training with Nick. They're facing away from us.

Levi turns toward the squad car, and I panic. What if they leave us here? What if the cougar comes back and brings his friends and family?

I open my mouth to call out but instead give a tiny squeak. I've heard mice make more noise. It's like a dream where you try to scream, but you can't. Grace looks like she's experiencing the same dilemma. As the flashlight beam moves farther away, Grace pounds her fist against the side of the shed. I join her, and a moment later, a flashlight beam is blinding us.

"Ouch." I try to shield my eyes.

Then the silence is so absolute I can hear the crickets over in Miller's pond.

Finally, Nick shakes his head and asks, "Why am I not surprised?"

7:30 p.m.

GRACE and I huddle together on my living room sofa. My older sister Sly tucks a soft blanket around us, then rushes off to make chamomile tea. Nick is speaking on his police radio to someone named Ranger Hawthorn.

Levi sprawls in the recliner across from us. "Dispatch says the phones are blowing up with calls about the cougar. You're the only ones who saw it, but lots of people recognized the screams." He nods at Nick. "It sounds like the trackers will head out as soon as possible."

Grace and I glance at each other and, in one voice, say, "Don't hurt it!"

Levi frowns and shakes his head. "They may not have much choice. He's been killing cattle on the mountain for the last month. He even tried to attack one of Mr. Marlin's horses last week, but a rifle shot scared him away.

"That he's come into town, well ..." Levi's voice trails off as we imagine what could have happened tonight.

Sly hurries into the room, carrying a tray with mugs of tea and peanut butter cookies she baked this afternoon. Nick finishes his conversation and sits beside her on the loveseat. As usual, a smile forms when I see Nick and Sly together. They've only been a couple for a few short weeks, but clearly, they're already in love.

I'm thrilled for Sly. When our parents died last year, she left college and took guardianship of me and our younger sister, Maggie, who recently turned 12. Even as our little family created a new normal, Sly's employer, Robert Sinclair, accused her of embezzlement. He threatened her with prison while Maggie and I faced the prospect of foster care.

Determined that wouldn't happen, I investigated on my own. I shiver, thinking of the dangerous situations I faced during that time.

Sly hands me a mug of tea. "I'm so glad God protected you and Grace tonight."

"Yeah, Jess's angels are earning their wings this year." Cole stands in the doorway, his expression a mix of concern and exasperation.

My heart flips at the sight of him, but I defend myself, "Hey, I was taking a walk and minding my own business."

Cole settles beside me and smooths a strand of hair from my face. "That's my point," he smirks. "You seem to find trouble even when you aren't searching for it. Heaven help us when you are."

I sip my tea, remembering those occasions when I searched for trouble.

Cole leans over to murmur, "I was teasing. I'm glad the cougar didn't hurt you two."

I smile at him. "I know, but what are the odds? Two girls out for an evening walk, stalked by a cougar."

To Sly, I offer, "You can have our interview for *The Voice of Justice*." Sly recently accepted a job as a photojournalist for our local newspaper, so the least I can do is give her an exclusive.

But, instead of looking excited, Sly bounces up, nearly knocking Nick's tea from his hand. Fortunately, Nick has excellent reflexes. It's probably a cop thing.

"Grace," Sly says. "Call your parents immediately. I don't want them to see this on Facebook. Word will be all over Justice in a few hours."

Grace's parents took her younger brother, Josh, to Missoula, and she's staying with us until they return later tonight.

Grace reassures her. "I used Levi's phone and called them on the way here."

"Oh my." Sly sinks into the love seat. "What did they say?"

"Mom cried a little, Dad said he would contact the wildlife officer tomorrow, and of course, Josh was jealous." Grace gives a slight grin, obviously remembering the excitement in her 10-year-old brother's voice.

"I'll call your mom myself," Sly assures Grace. "I feel terrible this happened while you were staying with us."

"Well, it's not like you drove up the mountain, grabbed the cat, and hauled him down here to terrorize teenage girls." Nick reaches for another peanut butter cookie. "So, why were you girls on the edge of town, anyway?" His matter-of-fact tone contrasts with his unwavering stare.

Grace glances at me, and I shrug.

"Exercise?" I offer.

Nick eyes my pointy-toed boots. "Right," he drawls. However, his tone suggests he doesn't believe that for one second. He reaches for another cookie and stands. "Levi and I are going to the sheriff's department and check the progress of the great cougar hunt. Everyone stick close to home until we get the all-clear, got it?"

I try not to be offended that when he says everyone, he stares at me.

Nick and Levi leave just as my younger sister, Maggie, rushes through the door. Her brown eyes are wide as she kneels beside me.

"Jess, are you guys, okay?" Maggie is petite and graceful, which makes her a talented gymnast. But now, shaking makes her clumsy as she reaches for me. I gather her into my lap, and Cole gently tugs at Maggie's auburn braid.

"She's okay, Magpie," he says.

After our parent's accident, Maggie struggled to accept their deaths. Then, a few weeks ago, she became more fearful as our family faced Sly's crisis. She's blossoming again, but we're very protective of her. I hope tonight's adventure doesn't trigger her nightmares.

I hold Maggie tight until I sense the stress leave her. Sly sits beside us and asks, "How did you know about the cougar? I wanted to tell you myself."

"Kylie Warren posted it on Instagram." Maggie muffles her words in my black sweater. Grace and I give each other an of-course-she-did look. No event in Justice is too insignificant for Kylie to document. A cougar in town will be a social media Christmas to her.

Sly gives Maggie's knee two gentle pats. "Jess and Grace are safe now. Go relax with a nice bath before bed."

I remember the times Mamma gave those two soft pats to show everything was fine. I'm sure Sly isn't even aware she did it.

Maggie studies me to make sure I'm whole and undevoured. Then she follows Sly upstairs, grabbing a cookie on her way.

Cole moves to the recliner and leans forward, his elbows resting on his knees. At 6 foot 2 inches, Cole fills up my dad's chair. He glances at me, Grace, and back to me. Then he nods at my boots and asks, "Exercise?"

Grace gives an unladylike snort, but otherwise leaves me to explain.

"Hey, it's no big deal. I needed to have a private conversation with Grace. Since it was a nice night, we took a walk. End of story."

Grace stares at me in dismay. "There was no *we* in that decision. You announced you had something important to tell me, and you insisted we keep walking. If you remember, I wanted to sit in my dad's warm car and talk. It's a proven cougar-free zone."

I gape at her. "Grace, what part of 'no one else can know' didn't you get?" I look pointedly at Cole, who raises an eyebrow.

"You needed to tell Grace something about me?" He asks. "Or about us?"

I'm distracted for a minute by the knowledge that Cole and I are an 'us.' Then I realize what he's asking. "No," I say, "not about you or ... us ..." I stammer, feeling my cheeks warm. "I just don't want Sly to know. Yet."

"Something dangerous." It's not a question, and Cole's frown is one I haven't seen since I risked my life several times to keep Sly out of prison. I haven't missed that expression at all.

"Doubtful," I say.

"So, yes," Cole says.

Grace turns to me, her blue eyes wide. "Jess, I didn't realize it was anything like that. I thought it upset you when Cole talked to Gwen Torres after church today."

I scowl at Grace, giving her a slight kick with my pointy toes. "Grace," I hiss. She glares back at me as she rubs her shin.

"This is a fascinating conversation, but let's go back to Jess doing something dangerous." Nick stands in the doorway, arms crossed over his chest.

"What are you, a ninja or something?" I mutter. "I thought you left."

"I did. Then I came back." Nick is a man of few words, but he makes them count.

As Sly descends the stairs, her face brightens when she sees Nick. He glances up, his expression softening. But if I think my sister will be a distraction, I don't know this sheriff's deputy.

"Jess is about to tell us some important information." Nick takes Sly's hand and tugs her to the loveseat.

"Oh?" Sly sounds puzzled but not alarmed, and my heart squeezes as I consider the grief she'll soon face. It's a heartache I've been carrying, alone, for a week.

"Jess?" Grace notices my tears and reaches for my hand. "I'm sorry."

She starts to say more, but I surge up, tired of carrying this knowledge alone. "Wait here. I'll be right back."

Their worried expressions haunt me as I race to my bedroom. I reach the closet and shove aside old backpacks and games until I pull out an ordinary manila file folder. Then, trembling, I return to the living room to break my sister's heart.

2

8:00 p.m.

I retake my seat, preparing for the storm of questions. But there's only silence as four pairs of eyes examine me, their gazes a blend of interest and apprehension. The manila file folder shakes in my hands, and I attempt to steady them.

"On the night I visited Robert Sinclair's office," I begin, but I'm interrupted by Nick's muttered, "broke into his office."

I glance at him in exasperation but continue. "I was searching for Sly's camera, which Robert had *stolen*," I say, emphasizing the word, "I discovered this in the file cabinet. Since our last name was on the tab, I grabbed it, assuming there might be information about Sly. I stuck it in my backpack, but I forgot about it after I found the camera. When I remembered the file, I read it and, well ..." My voice trails off as I hand the folder to Sly.

She accepts the folder with the tips of her fingers as if she's frightened it might explode. Nick moves closer to her, gently placing his hand on her shoulder. She opens the file to read, and the only sound is the *tick-tick* of Grandma's clock in the dining room. Moments later, Sly gives a strangled sob and lets the papers drop to the floor. Nick grabs them before they scatter.

Beside me, Grace and Cole move closer, an unspoken promise of protection, even though neither knows what we're facing.

Nick scans the papers, then glances up at me, his face a mask of control. "Jess, who else knows about this?"

I shake my head. "No one."

"Including us," Grace mutters, glancing at Cole in frustration.

I shift to her. "Remember, when my dad was a building inspector, he worked with Anthony Avery?"

Grace nods. "Anthony Avery, the guy who helped with Robert Sinclair's building scam."

"The same guy," Nick agrees. "And although the FBI has plenty of evidence against Sinclair, they still can't prove any crimes by Anthony Avery."

"Yet," I say.

"So, what's in the file?" Cole asks. He picks up my hand, and for the first time, I realize I'm trembling.

Nick paces the room, reminding me of the cougar we encountered earlier. "This is a report written by the girls' dad, Brian Thomas, detailing his suspicions about Anthony Avery. It accuses Avery of some serious and illegal actions. If the FBI could prove this, Anthony Avery would be in prison today."

"That's not the worst of it." Sly's voice cracks and tears gather, spilling down her pale cheeks.

"Right." Nick's grim tone and clenched jaw tell me he's read the entire letter. Everything.

"Mr. Thomas explains he was planning to wait before he sent the report, hoping to gather additional evidence. But something happened that concerned him enough to send it sooner."

Nick lifts Daddy's letter and reads, "Although I've tried to be discreet in my investigation, I'm concerned Avery suspects I know about his crimes. I encountered him at a building site today, and he made a statement that I took as a threat. As we walked around the area, I stumbled over some discarded lumber, and Avery said, 'Be very careful where you step, Brian. Accidents happen every day. You won't be any good to your family if you're injured.'"

Grace gasps and Cole tightens his grip on my hand.

Nick continues to read. "Although his words might sound innocuous, his tone and expression carried a definite warning. I must share the attached documents without delay to protect myself and my family."

I study my sister, who is staring at something only she can see. "Sly? You saw it, didn't you?" I ask.

At her nod, I move to kneel beside her chair. She lays her head on my shoulder, her tears soaking into my sweater.

"Saw what?" Grace whispers.

I swallow and shift to face our friends. "The date of the letter." I struggle to make the words sound matter-of-fact but fail. "Daddy wrote that letter two days before he and Mamma died in the car accident."

"I DON'T UNDERSTAND." Sly has been repeating those exact words for the past twenty minutes. She's not alone—none of us understands.

Nick continues to examine the papers. Besides Daddy's letters, the file holds receipts and a few photos. Remembering the pictures Sly took last month, I realize she unknowingly continued Daddy's investigation. Her photographs of Robert Sinclair and Anthony Avery led to Sinclair's arrest.

Grace sounds puzzled. "Why would Mr. Thomas send a report like that to Robert Sinclair?"

"He didn't," Nick says. "He addressed the report to," he flips through the pages and reads, "Clarence Delgado, the President of the Beaverhead County Building Inspector's Commission. But I don't understand why Robert Sinclair had it in his files."

Nick turns to Sly and me. "Would you two be all right with me taking these papers to the FBI? This information could be the piece of the puzzle they need."

When Nick says, "FBI," I shiver a little. I have a love/hate relationship with the FBI. They saved my life last month (love), but later low-key yelled at me for making that necessary (hate). But while I was with them, I became intrigued by the agents' energy and commitment to their work. My sentiments about the FBI are complicated, but I know if anyone can solve this, they can.

"I don't understand," Grace echoes Sly's earlier words. "Your parents died in a car accident when they skidded on a slippery highway." Grace's eyes apologize for even bringing up such a terrible memory.

"True," Nick answers before I can. "But it's worth investigating deeper, now that we've discovered this information." Nick stands and pulls Sly with him. "The timing could be a coincidence," he continues in a tone that says 'unlikely.' "But we need to settle the question."

As Nick and Sly walk to his squad car, I face Cole and Grace.

"Anthony Avery and Robert Sinclair killed my parents." I barely recognize my voice as I grit the words and swipe away angry tears.

"Jess." Grace joins me on the couch, rubbing my arm in a reassuring gesture. I try not to shrug her away, but I don't want comfort. I want revenge.

"Jess," Cole says my name too, but his tone is a caution. "We don't know that they caused the crash. And it's dangerous to make allegations without proof only the FBI can provide." He emphasizes the word only, and I realize he's advising me to stay out of the investigation. Let the professionals do their job.

"If we'd left it to the FBI, Sly would be in jail," I say, ignoring my previous awe at their efficiency. I stand to pace around the room with increased urgency. My hands wrap around my arms as I struggle to control myself. From what? Flying apart?

Cole's muscular arms envelop me, drawing me close. "Hey, take a breath," he whispers, and I gulp, recognizing a smart idea when I hear one. He pulls away, peering into my eyes. "Jess, I can't imagine what you're going through right now. Fury, confusion, hurt."

The tears I'd been fighting earlier win the battle and spill down my cheeks. When he sees them, Cole pulls me back to him and holds me for a long minute. The tightness eases from my body, and I sniff. "I need a tissue."

A feminine hand inserts itself between us, waving a wad of tissues. We pull apart, surprised to remember Grace is still in the room.

Cole smiles. "Grace to the rescue."

"Again." We laugh, saying the word in unison, and the tension eases.

The creaking of the porch steps alerts us that Sly is returning, and Cole and I separate as she enters the living room. She and Nick must have had a similar conversation, complete with the tears.

"This is the strategy," she announces. "Nick will give the file to the FBI for their investigation. He'll also examine the police record from the night of Daddy and Mamma's accident." Her voice breaks a little at these words, but then she says, "Nick asked me to deliver a message to you, Jess."

I perk up, anticipating an assignment.

"He said, and I'm quoting him, 'Stay. Out. Of. Trouble.'" Sly spaces each word, and I can hear Nick's voice in the message.

My cheeks flush, but I shrug. "Don't worry. I've learned my lesson. If they stick with it, I'll let the authorities handle the investigation. For now." Identical frowns crease three foreheads as Sly, Cole, and Grace take in my words. But before they challenge me, I add, "Besides, I have a new project."

"What's that?" Cole asks.

"I need to catch a cougar."

3

Monday, October 8
2:00 a.m.

D reams fascinate me. They're like movies that play in my mind, full of people I know and many I haven't met. I'm deep into a dream about a polka dot bear, a plaid moose, and a striped chipmunk having a picnic. They're arguing about who gets the last chicken drumstick, and I'm explaining it's mine, when I hear a snuffling noise.

Someone is crying. I scan the forest, trying to find the source of the noise. I lift a leaf to reveal a glittering raccoon. It gives me a relieved look and says, "You found me."

The sniffling continues, and as I search, the noise becomes louder. I lie down on the grass, crawling and patting the ground near my head.

"Hey!" Maggie yelps.

I sit up, abruptly leaving the peaceful forest, and find myself face to face with my little sister. Even in the moonlight, I can see the tears streaking her cheeks.

"Magpie," I say hoarsely, trying to orient myself back into reality. "What's wrong?"

"The cougar was watching me."

I gather her close and pull the blanket around us. "I'm sorry you had a bad dream. You can sleep here."

"It wasn't a dream."

"Of course, it was," I yawn. "There's no such thing as a polka dot bear."

Maggie gives me a strange look. "No." Her tone is impatient. "*You* were dreaming. Not me. The cougar was in the tree outside my window, watching me."

I smooth Maggie's auburn curls away from her face. "Honey, Grace screamed so loudly that cougar is in Canada by now. You were dreaming."

I snuggle down into the bed, already half asleep.

"You don't believe me." The hurt in her tone alerts me, and I face her, silently saying good night to my colorful forest friends.

"Maggie, it's not that I don't believe you. But it only makes sense you would dream about the cougar after everything that happened tonight. It's easy to assume dreams are real when you first wake up."

Maggie sits up and says, "The cougar was in my tree. When I came back from the bathroom, he was sitting there, staring directly at me. I made myself stay calm and came in here because I figured you would understand how scary he is." Maggie's tight voice and straight back show her offense.

I consider asking if she might have been sleepwalking but change my mind. Maggie has made a lot of progress overcoming the nightmares that began when our parents died. She's been seeing a counselor who helps all three of us navigate the stages of grief. Sleepwalking isn't a problem so far, and I have a sense if I suggest it, I will put a wall between us.

"Okay," I say. "I believe you." I shiver at the idea the cougar might have followed Grace and me to my home. Why? I don't know much about cougars, but I can't understand why he would bypass a town full of tasty morsels to follow me. But one glance at Maggie's face convinces me. She believes she saw the cougar.

The next moment a chill covers me when Maggie says, "You didn't mention he only has one eye."

"What?" I squeak.

"One eye." Maggie is calmer now that she has shared her terror with me, and she scoots down into the bed, wiggling to find a comfortable spot. "His left eye is missing."

7:30 a.m.

It's Grace's turn to drive, and, as usual, I'm running late. I snag a Pop-Tart from the kitchen and reach the porch as Grace's car pulls into the driveway.

"One second," I call, then jog down the stairs and around the side yard. As I approach the enormous tree outside Maggie's window, I tell myself to relax—there's no way the cougar was in this tree last night.

But he was.

The deep claw marks on the tree trunk prove it. For a second, I try to convince myself it was Mrs. Mendelssohn's cat who made the marks. Then I remember Peaches is declawed.

"His left eye is gone." I shiver as I remember Maggie's words from last night. That was one fact Grace and I hadn't told Maggie when we were reporting about our encounter with the cougar. Instead, we'd agreed it could cause more nightmares.

I trace my finger down the deep grooves in the tree.

"Whatcha' doin'?"

I yelp and drop my bookbag.

"Grace! Don't do that." I glower at her and pick up my bag.

"Do what?" Grace studies me as she munches an apple. For some reason, the fact she is eating a healthy breakfast while I'm currently digesting a chocolate Pop-Tart irritates me even more.

"Sneak up on me."

"You're kind of crabby this morning," Graces observes, taking another nibble of her apple. "Didn't you get any sleep?"

"Sorry." I sigh and take a deep breath. "No, I didn't sleep much."

Then I step aside, revealing the claw marks the cougar left in the tree outside my little sister's bedroom window.

Grace leans over to examine the gouges. "Are those what I think?"

"Yep." I use my phone to take several pictures for Nick. He may be able to find the animal's size based on how wide and deep the marks are. At least, I think I saw that on the Discovery Channel once.

"The cougar woke Maggie last night. At first, I thought she had a bad dream, but when she mentioned it only had one eye, I realized it was really there."

I slide my phone into my bag and follow Grace to her car.

"Weird," Grace says as she pulls out of the driveway. "What are the odds you would see a cougar, and that same night it would be outside your house? I mean, he had the entire town of Justice to terrorize."

I shrug, trying to shake off my uneasiness. "He probably visited a lot of places last night. I'm trying not to take it personally."

When I send the pic to Sly and Nick's phones, Nick texts back that a wildlife expert will take a look ASAP. I try to relax in the assurance the trackers are on their way to Justice.

But deep down, a nagging suspicion says this won't be my last encounter with the cougar.

12:00 p.m.

GRACE and I try to keep a low profile at school. But, thanks to Kylie Warren, news has spread about our encounter with the cougar last night. At lunch, we're surrounded by students who usually ignore us, begging for details.

"I can't discuss an ongoing investigation," I repeat something I heard Nick say once. Most people nod in acceptance and walk away.

Grace snickers. "I'm going to use that line the next time someone asks me a question I don't want to answer."

"Feel free," I say.

Terri and Macy join us, and Terri says, "Guess what?"

Before we can answer, Terri turns to her cousin and says, "Go on, Mace, you tell them."

Macy's rosy cheeks turn even brighter, but she gives a shy smile.

"Caleb and I are going to sing the national anthem at the game in two weeks."

"Wow, that's awesome," Grace says, and I nod.

"Which of you will play the guitar?" I ask.

"Caleb," Macy says. "At first, he wanted us to both play and sing, but I want to concentrate on my vocals since I'm singing harmony."

"It's going to be amazing," Terri says. "I heard them practice, and they sound so good together. Todd's going to video the performance and upload it to YouTube."

I unzip my bookbag and remove a piece of notebook paper and pen. When I place them in front of Macy, she looks confused.

"What's this for?"

"I want to be the first person ever to get your autograph." Macy's blush deepens, but when she sees I'm serious, she carefully signs her name.

"By the way, you made my mom cry in church yesterday," Grace says.

Macy frowns. "Why?"

Grace smiles and touches Macy's arm. "It was a good kind of

cry. When you and Caleb sang "I Can Only Imagine," she lost it. Your voices blend so beautifully."

Terri nods, "Yes, my mom had the same reaction."

I'm quiet, remembering my own jumbled emotions yesterday. When Pastor Jeff announced Caleb and Macy's duet, I was eager to hear them sing together for the first time. But when Caleb began strumming the song's melody, my heart pounded, and for a moment, I almost jumped up to run from the sanctuary.

But then Sly reached for my hand just as she took Maggie's on her other side. My sisters and I listened to the comforting words that the church choir had sung at our parent's funeral. Even as grief tried to drown me, the words gave me unwavering hope that we would see our parents again someday—in heaven.

Grace notices my silence and touches my hand. "Are you okay?" she whispers.

I nod, rapidly blinking hot tears from my eyes. Then, turning to Macy, I say, "I can't wait to hear you sing again. Cole and I will be on the front bleachers, cheering you on."

The conversation continues around me as I feel the sadness ebb away. For long months I fought my grief, thinking it was better to push it down. But I'm learning to let myself feel, even when it comes at unexpected times, like today.

"*Everyone grieves in their own way, Jess.*" Our counselor described the five stages of grief and is helping each of us find our own path. But there are times, like yesterday, when the Thomas sisters still grieve together.

I think about the letter Daddy wrote, and although I wonder if more pain is coming, I know we'll face the future the best way we can. Together.

4

Tuesday, October 9

At 3:15, I'm standing in front of my locker, debating if I should review for my upcoming American Lit test. Yes. Cole taps on the locker door.

"Hey," he says.

"Hey, yourself," I respond. I love our witty banter.

"Time for work." Cole reaches for my bag, and I release it.

Ben Hadley's ranch is five miles from town in the Pioneer Mountain foothills. When we arrive, Cole parks the pickup and says, "Tell you what. After I brush down Chieftain, I'll help you in the stables. We'll work together today—kind of like the buddy system."

I grin. "So, we're buddies now?"

Cole checks if anyone is in sight, then leans over and kisses the tip of my nose. "Oh yeah," he says with a grin. "The best."

I float to the stable. Since I'm still thinking of Cole's kiss—even if it was only on my nose—a few minutes pass before I remember the cougar. I glance around and assure myself that the doors are closed. Ben is taking extra precautions to make sure his horses are safe.

Cole joins me, and soon the stalls are clean, and the horses fed and watered.

At 5:30, we climb into Cole's truck to make the ten-minute trip home. But when we reach the end of the lane, Cole turns left instead of right.

"Hey, are you kidnapping me?" I ask.

"For a minute. We're stopping by the vet clinic to return some extra salve Ben didn't need."

I smile at the excitement in Cole's voice. After he graduates next spring, he will study to become a large animal veterinarian. Doc Anderson has already promised him a job when he graduates from college.

We approach the expansive pole building that houses the clinic, and I say, "I didn't realize Doc was adding on."

Cole's grin is a little self-conscious. "That's why I offered to return the salve for Ben. I wanted to show you where I'll work someday."

I echo his grin and follow him to the addition. I'm still smiling as we walk through the door. Then my smile dies as I come face to face with Anthony Avery.

WHEN I WAS ten years old, I played hide-and-seek with Cole and our friends, Todd and Terri. I had this great idea to climb a tree and watch the action happen below me.

Then I fell.

It wasn't a high fall—maybe five feet, but I landed hard on my back. I'll never forget that feeling of the breath leaving my body and the panic that it would never return.

Now, as I stare at the man who might have killed my parents, my breath disappears, and black spots flash around the corners of my eyes. I sway.

"Jess." Cole's muscular arm slips around my shoulders and tucks me to his side. "Steady, I've got you."

Anthony Avery studies me for a second, and I can tell when he realizes who I am. And unbelievably, he moves forward, hand extended.

"Ah, Ms. Thomas," he says. "My name is Anthony Avery. You may not remember, but I had the pleasure of working with your father. I was so sorry about the terrible accident that took your parents' lives."

Bile swills in my stomach. I imagine unloading what's left of Justice High's mystery lunch casserole onto Avery's polished, expensive shoes. I try to step forward for a better angle, but Cole doesn't budge.

"I know who you are," I grit out. Avery doesn't seem aware of my rudeness but continues to smile, combining fake sympathy and real menace in that expression.

"Yes, I suppose you do know me." The words are innocent, but they convey his true meaning. *'You know what I did and what I could do again.'*

Cole's arms tighten as if he's preparing to take a swing at Avery. As satisfying as that would be, it can't happen. The last thing I want is Anthony Avery's attention and menace turned on Cole.

Anthony Avery is my battle to fight.

We break the standoff when Doc Anderson comes through the door. Oblivious to the tension, he greets Cole like a long-lost son. Cole is often at the clinic, trying to learn from the aging veterinarian. Doc has said he'll retire the day Cole hangs his veterinarian diploma on the clinic wall.

"Cole, nice to see you. Hi there, Jess. I hope Cole brought you for a tour of the recent addition."

Doc turns to Anthony Avery and continues, "Mr. Avery here is from the Beaverhead building inspector's office. He's been overseeing the project since the day we poured the foundation."

My stomach lurches again when I think about Cole spending hours in a building that has Anthony Avery's very questionable stamp of approval. Who knows what dangerous building practices Avery tolerated in the project? I flash to my confrontation with Robert Sinclair a few weeks ago. Sinclair had been using faulty materials in the Justice Senior Center construction, aided by the suspect oversight of Anthony Avery. Sinclair faces a jail term for his part in the crime, but the FBI can't prove Avery's involvement. Yet.

Doc gestures for me to follow him, but Cole intervenes.

"I'm sorry, Doc, but Jess and I will have to take the tour another day. I stopped by to drop off the extra salve from Ben." Cole removes a tube from his pocket and hands it to Doc Anderson.

Doc accepts the medicine, a bemused frown on his face. "Um, sure, Cole. We can do this anytime."

Cole takes my hand, urging me to the exit, but Anthony Avery's voice stops us.

"It was great to see you, Jessica. I'm pleased you and your sisters are doing well. I'd like for that to continue."

The renewed tension in Cole alerts me to imminent disaster, so I grip his arm and pull hard.

"Let's go, Cole."

We're silent as we drive toward Justice, processing what just happened.

"That was a threat," I say the words in a flat tone I don't recognize.

"Yep." Cole's knuckles are white as his hands tighten on the steering wheel. His jaw clenches, and the vein throbs in the side of his neck.

I take a deep breath. "Well, I wish I could say Doc would be a valuable witness, but he doesn't have a clue, does he?"

Cole shakes his head. "Doc is one of the nicest guys you'll ever meet. While I told him about the situation with Robert Sinclair, he knows nothing about Avery's involvement. Doc trusts Avery to make sure the clinic is safe and up to code."

I nod, thinking of sweet Doc Anderson's trusting ways. I turn to Cole in alarm.

"We need another inspector immediately. If Avery is allowing faulty materials again, you and Doc could be in danger."

Cole sighs. "Most structural problems don't show up right away. But as years pass, trouble can start."

"Oh, great, So, about the time you're ready to start your career, the building could land on our heads?"

Cole pulls the truck into my driveway and shuts off the engine. When he faces me, I'm surprised a smile tugs at the corner of his mouth. Why is he smiling?

"*Our* heads?"

I feel my cheeks redden as I realize what I'm implying. In six years, Cole will be the veterinarian in Beaverhead County. Will we still be together? By the warmth in Cole's eyes, he likes the idea.

"Well, yeah. Who else is going to protect you when the walls fall down?"

But Cole doesn't smile at my attempted humor. Instead, he studies my face with an intensity I find intriguing.

"You will," he says. "And I'll protect you right back." Then he kisses me.

Kissing is still pretty new between us, but I'm always happy for the practice. Unfortunately, Maggie picks that moment to race across the yard, calling, "Jess and Cole, sitting in a tree K-I-S-S-I N-G." The last letter fades as she sees the look Cole shoots her way.

She raises her hands in mock surrender and grins, "Sorry, don't let me interrupt."

Cole climbs out and ruffles Maggie's hair, which has escaped her braid and flies around in russet waves. I grab my bag and join them in walking into the house.

My mouth waters at the spicy aroma coming from the kitchen. We're lucky Sly inherited Mamma's ability to cook. Cole's stomach rumbles, and I grin up at him. "Want to stay for dinner?"

He gazes longingly at the simmering pan of enchiladas Sly is removing from the oven.

"I wish," he says, and his stomach rumbles again. "But Mom has dinner waiting for me. Then I have to study for a biology exam." He gives Sly a quick grin and asks, "Rain check?"

"Of course." Sly steps to the counter and grabs a cupcake drenched in chocolate frosting. "Here, take this for the road."

He accepts the treat, and with a quick goodbye, he's out the door.

Sly left for work early this morning so she could spend the afternoon cooking and baking. As I chop the salad, I wonder when I should tell her about my run-in with Anthony Avery.

A knock sounds on the kitchen door, and Nick walks in wearing his deputy's uniform. He hangs his hat on a hook by the back door and calls, "Honey, I'm home."

Sly giggles, and I roll my eyes. No wonder she was motivated to cook and bake.

"Can you keep dinner warm just a while longer?" Nick asks, kissing Sly on the cheek. "Ranger Tyler Hawthorn from Montana Fish, Wildlife, and Parks is here to look at the markings Jess found on the tree."

"Of course," Sly agrees.

We find the ranger examining the red maple tree outside Maggie's window.

Nick makes the introductions, then asks, "What do you think, Tyler?"

"Well, I'd say you had a visit from one very large, male cougar." Ranger Hawthorn says. "See how high up the claw raking starts? It's nearly eight feet. So that means it was a long cat, and since the females are not that big—must be male."

"Was he just sharpening his claws?" Sly asks.

A look passes between Nick and Ranger Hawthorn, but the ranger says, "Sure, that could be."

"Or?" I ask, sensing another option.

"Sometimes male lions do claw rakings to, uh, mark their

territory." Ranger Hawthorn raises an eyebrow as if expecting a reaction.

Sly doesn't disappoint him. "What?" She squeaks.

Nick wraps his arm around Sly. "Tyler isn't saying that as fact, honey."

"Do you think the cougar followed me here because he smelled my shampoo?" This question has bothered me all day.

The ranger looks confused, then seems to catch on. "You mean from when you met him earlier that night?"

At my guilty nod, he shakes his head.

"Possibly, but compared to lions, cougars have a relatively weak sense of smell."

"It's rare to see a cougar near people, right?" Nick asks.

"Rare, yes. Unheard of, no." Ranger Hawthorn says. "There have been more reports of cougars coming into towns lately. Sometimes drought drives them, or maybe they've been displaced by more people living in the mountains. But whatever brought this fella to Justice, he's definitely not welcome. I'm trying to get ahold of True North. He's the best cougar tracker in the state. If this lion is Outlaw, True's the man for the job."

"Outlaw?" Sly and I ask together.

The ranger nods. "Yes, True North had a meeting with a cougar last year, up close and personal. The cougar attacked True's dog, Pepper. Killed her. True went after the cat with his knife and took out the cougar's eye in the fight. Course, True almost lost his own eye too."

I shudder. "The one-eyed cougar."

"Nick said you got a good look at the cat. You're sure he only had one eye?"

"Yes. And later, my sister, Maggie, saw him in this tree, and she said the same thing."

"Well, it's Outlaw then. True said he's never known a cougar to be so fearless. They usually avoid humans, but not this one." Ranger Hawthorn must see the alarm on our faces because he hurries to reassure us.

"Likely, Outlaw is long gone from Justice. True will pick up his trail and finish what he started. Just keep close to home for a few days, and it will all be over."

As Nick walks Ranger Hawthorn to his car, I look at the claw rakings again. I'm not sure if 'keep close to home' is the best advice.

When I meet Sly and Nick back in the kitchen, I remember my other concern. I take a deep breath and say, "I need to tell you something before Maggie comes down." Then I blurt out, "I saw Anthony Avery today, and I think he threatened me."

Nick's face reddens and he clenches his fists, but I explain how the meeting happened. "We didn't know he would be at the clinic," I assure them.

"Tell me again what he said to you," Nick growls, and I gulp, relieved I'm not the one he's mad at this time.

"He said he was glad my sisters and I are doing well, and he hopes that continues."

Sly's happy energy drains away, leaving her pale and shaking.

Nick prowls the kitchen. "I'll talk to Special Agent Slater at the FBI. He's handling the Avery case, and he needs to know about this. Of course, Avery will deny the threat if they ask him, but this is another piece of the puzzle."

He tugs Sly close. "It's going to be okay, sweetheart. If you all stay far away from him, you'll be fine."

"I don't want to worry Maggie with this. Can we keep it between us?" Sly asks.

Nick and I nod, and Sly turns, placing a bowl of chips and salsa on the table. Then she squares her shoulders, lifts her head, and gives a shaky smile.

"Dinner's ready."

"Magpie," I call up the stairs. "Let's eat," and a moment later, she glides into her chair.

We hold hands as Nick says grace, and as he prays, I whisper a prayer of my own.

"Deliver us from evil."

5

Wednesday, October 10
3:15 p.m.

"Hey, could we stop by the Ellison's house on the way to BOB tonight?" Grace leans against the locker beside me and drops her book bag. The thud it produces makes me worry there will be a crack in the floor when she picks it up again.

I smile in anticipation of meeting up with our friends at youth group tonight. Bunch of Believers, affectionately known as BOB, is the highlight of my week.

"Sure. Let's grab food at the Dairy Barn first and take a treat with us for the twins." I slam my locker door, and we move to the exit, dodging our classmates who possess the same goal. Escape.

"I'll text Sly and make sure she doesn't need the car." I grab my phone and send the text, but I'm surprised when she calls instead of texting back.

"You can use the car," she agrees. "But please be careful and check in a few times while you're out."

Something in her voice alerts me, and I ask, "Sly, what's wrong? Did something happen?"

"Not exactly. But when I was walking home from work today, I got this weird feeling someone or something was watching me. I was running by the time I hit the porch steps."

Goosebumps rise on my arms and guilt swamps me.

"I'm sorry, I shouldn't have asked for the car this morning."

"Jess, it was a beautiful day, and you know I usually enjoy that walk. This is not on you. Be careful and text me a few times this evening. Please."

I agree and end the call.

Grace is practically vibrating as she asks, "What? Is Sly okay?"

I tell Grace about Sly's walk home, and she says, "Now that's just creepy. Do you think it was Anthony Avery? Or the cougar?" Grace shivers. "Imagine two pairs of eyes watching you from the shadows."

I nibble my lip, considering, as we walk to Sly's Honda. "One and a half," I say.

"Huh?" Grace's forehead wrinkles a little in confusion.

"Not two pairs of eyes," I explain. "The cougar is missing one eye."

WE DROP Grace's backpack at her house and check in with her mom. Mrs. Compton recently opened her own interior decorating company, and she's in the middle of a Zoom meeting with a client. She glances up as Grace and I enter the room, making sure we stay out of camera range.

Grace uses sign language to explain our plans to her mom. Mrs. Compton nods, smiles, and blows us a kiss. I grin, realizing that's the only part of the conversation I understand. Grace's Grandma Compton is deaf, and the entire family often uses sign language to communicate.

As we leave the house, I ask, "How did you tell her everything in only those few movements?"

"I signed, 'food, twins, BOB, home.'" Grace slides into the passenger seat and pulls down the mirror to study her face. She frowns, and I'm sure she's inspecting the light freckles that dance across the tops of her cheeks and nose.

Grace is not a fan of her freckles, although I think they're cute. She fluffs her red-blonde curls, then digs in her purse, grabs a lipstick, and applies a light gloss.

I raise an eyebrow. "You won't see Kellen until we get to the BOB meeting. Why mess with lipstick now?"

Ever since Grace and Kellen attended homecoming together, Grace has upped her makeup game.

She shrugs and slides the lipstick back into her purse. "I have chapped lips."

"Uh-huh." I grin and pull out of the driveway. Next door, Janey and Joey Ellison are using chalk to draw on their sidewalk. Mrs. Ellison perches on the front step, watching them with an eagle eye.

Grace waves as we drive by. "I was going to tell them we're bringing a treat from the Dairy Barn, but I've learned the hard way that with the twins, a surprise is better than a promise."

"Oh yeah," I agree. "Otherwise, they'll bug their mom every five minutes, asking when we'll be back. Surprise is always the better choice."

We buy the treats and return to the Ellison home. The front door is standing open, but the screen door is locked. At our knock, Mrs. Ellison's voice calls, "Coming." A moment later, she flips the lock open.

"Hi, girls, c'mon in." She laughs as she engages the lock again. "You must think I'm silly. I mean, the cougar can't open doors, right?" She leads us into the family room, where the twins are busy creating chaos.

Toys litter the floor, and several colorful throw pillows have been ... well, thrown. One leans against the bookcase while another blocks our entry into the room.

Mrs. Ellison reaches to swipe it up without breaking stride.

"Look who's here," she sings out, and the twins turn to stare in surprise. Then they hurtle themselves at us, nearly knocking Grace to the floor. I see them coming, so I brace for impact.

"Hi guys," I say, reaching out to steady Grace. "We brought you treats from the Dairy Barn."

Too late, I wonder if Mrs. Ellison might want the twins to save the ice cream until after dinner. I give her an apologetic wince, but she smiles. "You know, I expect we can bend the rule once in a while."

Janey gives an excited squeal and grabs Grace's arm, pulling her toward the kitchen. I hold up the ice cream bar I brought for Joey, and he glances at it but shrugs. "Maybe later. I need more pwactice." The twins turned five last week, and Joey celebrated by losing his first tooth. He looks and sounds adorable.

"Practice for what?" I ask, noticing the toy bow and arrow he is clutching in his hands.

"I'm gonna twack the tiger." His words are solemn.

Confused, I ask, "Joey, do you mean the cougar?"

Joey nods and turns to fit the arrow into the bow. After a second, he succeeds, but the arrow falls to the floor when he pulls the string. His lip trembles, but he picks up the arrow and tries to notch it again.

"Here, let me help you." Laughter comes from the kitchen as Janey enjoys her ice cream treat. But her twin has more important things on his mind.

Joey watches as I show him how to fit the arrow into the notch. The soft rubber of the bow and arrow makes it hard to accomplish the task. But, after a few tries, Joey masters the art, and the arrow flies into the pillow.

"Great job!" I declare. "You've earned yourself some ice cream."

Joey nods and grabs my hand. "Yep," he says and shows me his sweet, gap-toothed grin. "I'll pwactice more after dinner."

Later, we drive to Pastor Jarrod and Anna's house where BOB meets each week.

I share with Grace about Joey's determination to track the cougar.

"I wish I could post a video of him saying, "I'm gonna' twack the tiger.' But I doubt the Ellisons want Joey to go viral."

"No kidding," Grace agrees. "When Janey was eating her ice cream, Mrs. Ellison told me the parents at the twins' preschool are helping during outdoor playtime. They don't want the kids to miss being outside, but they don't want to meet the cougar, either. There were as many parents as kids on the playground this morning."

"I hope this True North tracker will get here soon," I say. "The entire town is on edge."

BOB has already started when Grace and I arrive, and we find a spot on the floor in front of the leather loveseat. Terri and Macy are sitting there, and they let us lean back against their knees to get comfortable.

Across the room, Cole gives me a slight nod and smile, and I return the favor. Grace glances around, and when she spots Kellen near the dining room, she relaxes and settles in to enjoy the evening.

Pastor Jarrod steps into the middle of the room and does a 360. "Excellent, we have a full house tonight."

He glances at Grace and me, and unease prickles along my neck. I sense Grace tense up too, and I realize we are thinking the same thing. *Please don't ask me to pray.*

"I'm sure everyone is eager to question Jess and Grace about their recent adventure with the cougar. But let's save that for later so we can dive into tonight's lesson."

Grace and I sag back against Terri and Macy's knees, relieved we've avoided being the center of attention.

"Tonight, we're going to have a brief history lesson." Some groans sound around the room, but I straighten up a bit, intrigued. History is my favorite subject.

Pastor Jarrod moves to lean against the stone fireplace and asks, "Who knows how Justice, Montana got its name?" Quiet descends, and in the corner, someone, I suspect Caleb, hums the tune to *Jeopardy* while everyone laughs.

"I appreciate the sound effects, Caleb," Pastor Jarrod says, confirming my suspicion. "Do you have the answer?"

Caleb shakes his head, and Pastor Jarrod scans the room. "Anyone?"

Behind me, Macy shifts, and in her soft southern drawl, she says, "I know."

I turn to peer up at Macy, surprised. She and her mother left Tennessee and moved to Justice last month. It's odd that she would have the answer.

"I Googled it when I first came here," Macy explains. "Justice is a cool name, and I thought it must have a story to go with it."

"Would you be willing to share the story with us?" Pastor Jarrod asks.

"Sure." Macy clears her voice. "About 150 years ago, miners discovered gold in Bannack, Montana."

I give a slight start when Macy says Bannack, remembering my recent, unwanted trip to the local ghost town. Mark Crowley, another senior at Justice High, had been angry at Cole and tried using me to hurt him. The results had almost been tragic. Shivering, I glance over at Cole, and he meets my gaze. Although we've worked through the events of that night, the memory still makes me uneasy.

Macy continues, "Bannack grew quickly with miners, and soon 3,000 people were living there." Others in the room reflect my surprise as we consider the deserted town we know. It doesn't seem possible that anyone lived in Bannack, let alone 3,000 people.

"The miners moved their gold from Bannack to Virginia City, and soon outlaws began robbing them. They often killed anyone who resisted. When Sheriff John Plummer came to Bannack, he said he could end the robberies. But they got even worse, and eventually, people suspected that Sheriff Plummer was the ringleader of the robbers.

Some men decided that the only response was to hang the sheriff."

"Please don't say they killed him here in Justice?" Tiffany Landreth asks with a shudder.

Macy shakes her head.

"No, some settlers opposed the hanging, and they argued with the others. The argument went so deep that they left Bannack and started their own town. They named it Justice."

"Excellent." Pastor Jarrod stands and moves to the middle of the room again. "So, tell me, what do you think the word justice means?"

Caleb hums again, but a nudge from Kellen stops him.

"When Terri eats the last of my Lucky Charms, I want justice." Todd grins, and behind Grace, Terri groans.

"First, those are not *your* Lucky Charms. They belong to the family." Terri makes air quotes. "I'm part of the family, ergo, I can eat them."

I watch as Caleb pulls out his cellphone and types, probably Googling the word *ergo*.

"Okay, let's go with this," Pastor Jarrod says. "Todd, what would be justice for Terri eating all the cereal?"

In the corner, Caleb mutters, "Dump a gallon of milk on her head."

Pastor Jarrod appears startled then turns to Anna. "Remind me not to touch any of Caleb's food."

Macy says, "He could ask me where Terri keeps her secret stash of Twix bars, and he could eat them all. And share with me, of course."

Terri turns to glare at her traitorous cousin.

"Don't worry. I'll never tell," Macy promises with a grin.

Todd's expression is interesting as various scenarios must play out in his mind, but he settles for a BOB-approved response. "She'd have to get me some more."

"Great answer," Pastor Jarrod agrees. "That feels like justice. Terri should replace the cereal."

Behind me, Terri mutters, "The cereal belongs to all of us."

"Now, let's take Caleb's somewhat disturbing response and consider it. Would dumping a gallon of milk all over Terri be justice? Or would it be revenge? What's the difference?"

"Not only are they out of cereal, now they're out of milk too," Grace observes.

We all laugh, then Cole says, "I think the difference is the motive. Anger and the desire to punish the other person motivates revenge. Justice is more focused on balancing the scales, making it right and fair again."

Pastor Jarrod nods. "Exactly. For instance, what would happen if we chose a jury from the friends and family of a victim? Do you think the accused murderer would get a fair trial?"

"No way," Kellen says. "Anger would motivate their verdict."

"Yes," agrees Pastor Jarrod. "Anger fuels revenge but fairness guides justice."

That statement catches my attention, and in a moment of honesty, I wonder, can I let go of my desire for revenge? Do I trust God to bring Anthony Avery to justice?

I'm aware of the discussion continuing around me, but my thoughts go to my conversation with Sly earlier tonight. Sly is not easily frightened, and I believe someone—or something— was watching her this afternoon. I grasp my sweating palms together to disguise their shaking as anger roils through me.

Was Avery watching Sly, attempting to intimidate her? Or was the cougar continuing his curious stalking of the Thomas sisters? I take a deep breath, trying to calm my racing thoughts. Then I close my eyes and ask God to protect us—Sly, Maggie, and me—from man and beast.

6

Thursday, October 11
11:45 a.m.

"Scoot over." The noise level is deafening as the entire student body of Justice High School clatters its way onto the gymnasium bleachers. Grace nudges my hip with her bookbag, and I slide down the aluminum bench, allowing her to join me.

I scan the faces across the expanse of the gym, where the juniors and seniors sit. Grace interrupts my search for Cole when she pokes me in the ribs.

"Hey," I complain, turning to frown at her. "What was that for?"

"Look." Grace ignores my complaint and points to a group of adults gathered near the rolling stage. "Who's that?"

I glance down where Principal Evans stands with Nick and a man I don't recognize. The word grizzled pops into my mind. He could be anywhere between 50 and 70 years old. I can't tell because his gray hair is sticking out in every direction under his battered hat. Deep lines cover his sun-weathered face, but none look like they were caused by smiling too much.

Before I can respond, Principal Evans climbs the three short steps and crosses the platform to the microphone. He gives an experimental tap that elicits ringing feedback. He frowns at Willard Shockley, the AV club's sole member, and waits while Willard adjusts something on the soundboard, then gives a thumbs up.

"All right, students, settle down." That's the first warning. Experience tells us Principal Evans will repeat that phrase two more times before he reverts to his Marine sergeant days and growls, "Knock it off!"

When that ritual is behind us, Principal Evans continues, "As most of you know, two students spotted a cougar near our town." A low howling erupts from the corner of the gym where the sophomore boys sit. Since I personally experienced the lion's scream, I could give them some tips on authenticity.

Principal Evans levels them a stare that I'm sure demoralized many a Marine, and I wonder if his next words will be "drop and give me 50." Regrettably, the boys calm down, depriving us of that entertainment.

He continues. "Today, we have with us Truman North, a well-known tracker who will give us some instructions on how you should respond if you encounter the cougar. His advice might save your life, so please give him your attention." Principal Evans steps aside and motions for the grizzled man to approach the mic, tossing one more warning glance toward the sophomore boys.

Truman North is a legend in Beaverhead County. I remember Daddy talking about him a few years ago when a bear had been harassing hikers, tearing up their tents, and stealing their food. The bear hadn't injured anyone, but park rangers had called True to find the bear and help relocate him. I remember Daddy calling True North a 'character.'

"Cougar. Mountain Lion. Puma. Different names, same animal. But I call him Outlaw." The gruff voice isn't loud, but it still silences the room. "See, I know this cat. I've been tracking him for a year. He gave me this." True removes his wide-brimmed hat, and audible gasps echo as we view the lion's handiwork—or claw-work.

There are two deep gouges carved in his temple. White, raised ridges of scar tissue run from his hairline to his eyebrow. A longer scar travels within an inch of his right eye, ending at his cheekbone.

True waits for silence and continues, "Outlaw pretty near took my eye. I did take his." Nausea rises as I remember the gaping hole where the cougar's left eye had been. There was no mistake. Grace and I met Outlaw face-to-face.

"Mountain lions rarely come into town, but Outlaw isn't your typical lion. The girls who met him the other night were lucky." Now, hundreds of eyes fixate on Grace and me, and together we slide down and attempt invisibility. True continues, and since the words 'attack' and 'deadly' are in the following sentence, our fifteen seconds of fame are over.

"I'm gonna' give y'all some tips on how to avoid a deadly attack." Nick is standing beside True, and at these words, a fleeting frown crosses Nick's face. I imagine he was hoping True would be a voice of calm and reason. But that doesn't appear to be True North's plan.

Before Nick can interrupt, though, True goes on, "Now, a lion moves around between dusk and dawn. You'll want your pets and little ones inside since a cougar can grab them quicker than lightning, and you'll never see them again."

Nick moves forward in response to the crowd's gasps. "Let's take precautions without resorting to panic." Nick's calm voice settles us, and True appears to remember he's talking to school kids and softens his tone.

"Yeah," he says gruffly. "Like the deputy said, no need to panic. Keep your outside lights on, and stick close to home for a few days. Outlaw and I are gonna have our reckoning." The grim determination in his words sends a chill over my arms, and I shiver a little.

"If you spot the lion," True continues, "do not run away! He'll chase you for sure, and since cougars can run up to 40 miles an hour, he'll catch you. Guaranteed."

He stretches the word into three syllables. "Guar. An. Teed."

"Make yourself look as big and scary as possible, and if there's a stick or rock nearby, pick it up, always facing the lion. Don't make any sudden moves. Back up, but never turn your back. If you think he might attack, wave your arms, yell, and throw anything you have at him."

Nick steps forward and leans into the mic. "Thank you, Mr. North. I'm sure we will all take every precaution."

A few minutes later, the rumble of feet on metal benches echoes through the gym. We dismiss for the lunch break, where talk of Outlaw dominates the conversation.

"Did you hear what happened?" Terri and Macy slide in beside me at lunch.

Grace glances up from studying her plate of food. Her brows draw together as she asks, "What do you think this is?" She pokes at a glob of noodles dotted with mushy peas and soggy potato chips.

"Tuna casserole." Terri points to the menu posted near the serving station.

"I know what it's supposed to be," Grace agrees. "I like tuna casserole. I don't think this is that."

"What happened?" I ask Terri, abandoning Grace to her casserole fate.

"Outlaw attacked Mrs. Fielding's neighbor's dog."

"Wait, I heard he attacked one of Troy Emmon's baby goats," Macy says.

"Maybe it was both." Grace covers the uneaten glob with a napkin. "Mrs. Fielding is two streets over from me." Grace nibbles on her lower lip, and I assume it's worry and not hunger churning in her stomach.

"He's in town," Terri confirms. "Sarah Matthews said her dad spotted Outlaw digging in their garbage last night."

Grace pushes her tray away, and I see our future written in her eyes. Our first stop after school will be the Dairy Barn.

News of Outlaw swirls around us all day. The teachers require Grace and me to describe our adventure several times in front of the entire class. By three o'clock, I'm desperately hoping True North catches Outlaw soon before Grace and I are forever labeled "The Puma Posse."

I HAVE a hard time finding a parking spot at the Dairy Barn. It will close for the season in a few days, and people are trying to grab all the Dairy Barn goodness they can while there's still time. We place our orders and opt to sit at one of the picnic tables outside. There are only two booths inside, so it doesn't pay to keep the restaurant open during the cold months.

I give my money to Grace and grab a table in the sun. I pull my denim jacket around my shoulders as an unexpected chill sweeps through me. I glance around, anticipating either Anthony Avery or Outlaw. Maybe both.

But all I see are the vivid scarlet, cinnamon, and amber colors that decorate the trees of Justice. A sudden longing for my mother swamps me, and I choke back a sob. Mamma loved fall. There were many afternoons when she and I would sit on the swing and soak up the gorgeous colors. She often quoted, "Autumn shows us how beautiful it is to let things go."

I blink away tears, remembering those wise words. Those were days of innocence before I had anything to let go of. Before Anthony Avery.

As Grace approaches with our food, she studies me for a minute but doesn't say anything. That's one of the qualities I love about Grace. She knows when to push and when to let me be. I give her a grateful smile that encompasses more than the chili cheese fries she places in front of me.

I'm about to attack my food when conversation from the

next table catches my attention. Three older men are sitting at the table, licking ice cream cones with the abandon of five-year-olds.

"Yep, that Outlaw is a killer." Ed Hopkins used to own the hardware store in Justice. When he retired, he joined his two friends, Jack Bixby and Terrell Ford, who always sat outside his store, offering advice and gossip to whoever stopped to talk. Somehow, they acquired the nickname "The Three Wise Men," and we can find them at the Dairy Barn several times a week. This must be our lucky day.

I scoot closer, trying to listen. If anyone knows what's happening in the search for Outlaw, it will be the Wiseguys. Wise men. Whatever.

"Yep, I think Sheriff Herman is putting too much stock in True North being able to track that cougar. I mean, they've been circling each other for close to a year. He should have finished it by now." At around seventy, Terrell Ford is the oldest of the men. He retired several years ago when his son, Toby, took over the family-owned Chevy dealership.

They have a big sign at the edge of town that declares, "You should own a Chevy. Just ask a Ford!" I smile as I remember driving by the sign with my family. My dad would often chuckle and say, "Marketing Magic."

I'm brought back to the present by Jack Bixby's deep voice.

"Could be neither one wants to end it." His tongue swipes a drip on the side of his cone. "Maybe they enjoy the hunt too much."

"I don't think so," Ed says. "Did you see True at the council meeting this morning? He didn't look like a fellow having a good time."

"Well, I'd scowl too if Mayor Cranston was yelling at me like that." Jack focuses on another drip as his sticky hand obliterates the wafer. You'd think this was his first ice cream cone.

"The mayor is feeling pressured by the rancher's association and the town council to get this resolved ASAP." Terrell Ford pops the rest of his cone in his mouth and wipes his lips with a paper napkin. "Darren Barnes almost lost his prize mare to Outlaw last week. Now the cougar is stalking teenage girls right here in town. We need to do something."

Grace shifts closer to me, and by the tension in her body, I know she's heard the conversation too.

"My Janet came home from her book club today, all upset because Gladys Washington's little terrier, Taffy, was barking all through their meeting." Finally, Jack decides the cone is too much work and tosses it in the nearby trash can. "They were sure Outlaw would be waiting to pick them off, one by one when they left."

"Humph," Ed snorts. "That pipsqueak barks at his own shadow. Taffy. What kind of name is that for a dog, anyway?"

As the men move away, Grace touches my arm, and I jump.

"Hey, it's just me."

I settle back on the bench and sigh. "Sorry, but any talk of that cougar weirds me out."

"I know, me too. I can't believe we came face to face with him and lived to tell about it."

"It's also creepy that he left those scratches on the tree outside Maggie's window and maybe stalked Sly. I mean, what are the odds that all three Thomas sisters have a close encounter with a cougar?"

"I think you've met your quota." Grace nudges my chili cheese fries closer. "Are you going to finish those?"

I glance at the plate, and nausea washes over me. "Nah, go ahead."

Grace reaches for a fry and shakes her head. "Nope, I can't do it either. C'mon, we've procrastinated enough. Let's go conjugate some French verbs."

"Yippee," I say with minimal enthusiasm and maximum sarcasm. "I thought you'd never ask."

7

Friday afternoons have their own kind of energy. At 2:45, you're sitting in French class, conjugating verbs, and the air feels so thick you're about to suffocate. Then, ten minutes later, the bell rings, carrying the sweet breath of freedom.

Grace and I are swept along in the wake of our classmates. Sounds of escape fill the hallway, with locker doors slamming and sneakers racing toward the exit. It's like we're all afraid another bell will ring, and Principal Evans will announce he's canceled the weekend, and everyone must return to class.

Cole is waiting by my locker when Grace and I arrive. He smiles at me, then turns to Grace.

"I'm glad I caught you before you left. Ben Hadley called and asked if I know anyone who might work at a birthday party tomorrow at the ranch. Would you like to earn some extra cash?".

I open my locker and exchange my book bag for the duffel holding my work clothes.

"It'll be fun," I encourage Grace. "You can go with me. I'll be helping Cole lead the ponies for the rides. Ponies and cake, what better way to spend a Saturday afternoon?"

"Will there be little kids?" Grace asks.

"That's kind of the purpose," Cole teases.

"Okay. I could use the money for those boots I want. I'm in."

"Great," Cole turns to me. "We'd better get on the road. We'll have extra work to get the shelter ready for the party tomorrow."

I leave Grace with a promise to see her at 10:00 a.m. the next morning. Minutes later, Cole and I are traveling up the mountain. While he drives, I scan the landscape. As usual, the mountains draw my attention first, with their white-tipped peaks rising above the tree line. Then I turn to study the grassy banks along Grasshopper Creek.

"What are you doing?" Cole asks.

"Nothing," I'm self-conscious and a little embarrassed by my obsession with the cougar.

But I don't fool Cole. "I haven't heard of any sightings lately. Try to relax. I mean, it's rare to encounter a cougar in the wild once, let alone twice. I assume you've filled your quota. For your lifetime."

"Grace said the same thing," I agree. "Except Outlaw climbed Maggie's tree in the middle of the night," I remind him and shudder. "I'll be glad when he's gone. I keep feeling like someone's watching me."

Cole grins, and I know he's trying to lighten the mood. "You are being watched. By me."

My cheeks flush. "Well, I believe that's part of your job description. You're my boyfriend." My heart flutters when I say the words, hardly believing they are true.

Cole reaches over to squeeze my hand. "I am," he says, and just like that, I forget the one-eyed cougar.

A few minutes later, my mood plummets when we park near the stables, and I spot a white Mazda parked apart from the other vehicles.

"What is Amy Sinclair doing here?" I ask. "Did you know she was riding today?" I try not to sound accusing, but I must fail because Cole's jaw tightens.

"I didn't, but you had to realize you'd meet her here again." He climbs out and walks around to grab his duffle from the truck bed.

I slip out carefully as if putting my feet on the ground will bring Amy running. It's bad enough I have to see her at school, but the ranch is my safe place, and Amy is *not* safe.

As we walk, I remember my last encounter with Amy in the stable yard. Last month, Amy's Uncle Robert had Sly arrested for a crime she didn't commit. Amy had deliberately taunted me, and I lost my temper. Our confrontation ended with Amy in the dirt and Cole carrying me to his truck. Not my finest moment.

"Are you going riding with her?" I ask.

"Nope." Cole walks into the tack room and brings out the bucket and pitchfork. "Let's change, and after we clean the stalls, I'll ask what Ben needs us to do at the shelter." He opens his mouth to say more, then shakes his head and stomps off.

I enter the women's restroom to change, racking my brain to understand why he sounds irritated.

Amy has been a problem between us for over a month. First, she seemed to assume Cole was hers to claim, although they'd only exercised horses together once in the past month. Then she accused Sly of a crime she didn't commit. Of course, my reaction hadn't been very Christ-like, and I've even thought about apologizing for attacking her. But seeing her car here now is bringing back all my old insecurities.

I pull on my boots and begin working. Cole is already busy in Chieftain's stall, and I take a minute to glance at them. They are both beautiful. Cole wouldn't like that description, but it's the truth.

Faded jeans, scuffed boots, and a denim shirt, Cole takes my breath away. It's so strange because we've known each other since we were in grade school, but now I see him with fresh eyes.

I believe he sees me like that too, but when Amy is around, I can't help but compare my short, curvy figure to her tall, willowy one. My auburn hair waves around my face no matter how tightly I secure the braid down my back. Amy's silver-blonde hair is perfect every time.

As if thinking of Amy calls her to my side, there she is, in all her glory. Today she's wearing shredded jeans and a yellow sweater that must have cost over $200.00. I tighten my lips and focus on cleaning Penelope's stall, resisting the urge to 'accidentally' toss the soiled straw in Amy's direction.

Amy ignores me, walking past with a sniff as if she smells something unpleasant. Ha! She's in a horse stable. What does she expect?

She makes a beeline for Cole and says with a sweet tone that makes my teeth ache, "Hi Cole. Could you help me saddle Damsel? I decided to ride at the last minute, so I didn't bring any old clothes. I'd hate to ruin my brand-new sweater."

Oh, brother, how obvious can she be? Surely Cole can see she's flirting with him again. And right in front of me. I snort, and Penelope echoes the sound. I pat the mare's neck, calming her, and add that to my grievances with Amy. She made me scare sweet Penelope.

I hear Cole answer, "Sure," as he follows Amy out of the stable. Taking a deep breath, I count to twenty in Sioux. Cole taught me how to count in Gaelic, Sioux, and Spanish. I can also make it to 12 in French, although Madame Fellini frowns at my pronunciation.

Since counting in another language takes longer, Cole says this is a perfect system for calming my temper. I've been practicing my Sioux, so I start there. But I only reach 15 when Cole returns to Chieftain's stall.

"That was quick." I'm immediately mad at myself for saying anything, but he was gone for less than two minutes. Even Cole isn't that adept at saddling a horse.

"I introduced her to Keith, and he said he'd be happy to help her." A smile plays around the corners of Cole's mouth, and I realize Amy's manipulation didn't fool him at all.

We spend the following hour grooming Pebbles and Rocky for their gig tomorrow. The party is my first event at the ranch, and I'm looking forward to leading the kids around on the ponies. That will be a lot more fun than my usual Saturday chore of mucking the stalls.

By 6:00 p.m., we're back on the road to Justice, tired, a little smelly, but satisfied everything is ready for tomorrow.

"What are your plans tonight?" Cole asks.

"Well, since your brother is taking my sister out to dinner, I offered to hang with Maggie tonight. She said something about painting our nails." I hold out my hands to display my dirty and jagged fingernails.

"Good luck with that," Cole grins.

"Oh, you'll be amazed when you see me tomorrow. Maggie has a gift."

Cole stops the pickup in my driveway, and I grab my bag. I turn to say goodbye, wishing we could kiss but feeling grimy. Cole appears to read my mind as he reaches out to tug gently at my braid.

"Tomorrow, cowgirl," he says.

I rub my cheek against his hand, then hop from the truck, smiling because I have a promise of tomorrow. With Cole.

7:00 p.m.

HOLDING OUT MY HANDS, I examine my nails, neatly shaped and shining with clear polish.

"I wish you'd let me put a color on your nails," Maggie gripes as she sorts through the basket of nail polish. She removes an eye-popping lime green color and puts it on the table between us.

"Nuh-uh," I say, moving back from the table. "That's a hard pass."

"Relax." Maggie shakes the bottle then carefully opens the lid. "This is for me. Can you paint my nails?"

"Sure, but I can't guarantee there won't be smudges. I'm not very good at this."

"Don't worry," Maggie splays her hands on the table in preparation. "I'll clean up any mess you make."

"Okay, you asked for it." I take the brush, dip it in the lacquer, and then tentatively paint a tiny streak on the nail of her little finger.

Maggie rolls her eyes but doesn't say anything, although I'm sure I can hear her thoughts loud and clear. *'This is gonna take FOREVER.'*

We're quiet for a few minutes as Maggie wisely lets me concentrate on the job.

"Do you think Sly and Nick are going to get married?"

My hand jerks, and Feelin' Just Lime streaks across Maggie's finger and up to her second knuckle.

"Hey!" She grabs a paper towel and scrubs at the polish.

"Sorry." I put the brush back in the bottle. "But it's your fault for asking that question at the wrong time."

"Is there going to be a right time to ask?"

I sigh. "I don't know Magpie. They've only been together for a few weeks. It's way too soon to think about marriage."

Maggie removes the brush and begins to apply the polish to her nails. "They're in love." Her words are matter-of-fact.

I start to tease her and say, 'Now what do you know about love?' but stop myself. She knows it when she sees it.

"Probably," I say. "But maybe we should give them time to figure it out on their own."

At first, Maggie doesn't respond, but then she says, "What if Nick doesn't want us?"

For a moment, I'm confused, but then I carefully take the brush from her fingers and return it to the bottle. Her head is still lowered, and when she looks up, I see tears gleaming in her eyes.

"Oh, Maggie," I say and move to gather her onto my lap. At twelve, she is still petite and barely weighs 75 pounds. "Nick's a smart guy. I'm sure he understands we're a package deal." I smile, trying to reassure her.

"That's easy for you to say," she sniffs. "You'll be gone to college in two years. Nick and Sly will be stuck with me a lot longer."

"Maggie!" I can't hold back my shock. "No one is *stuck* with you. Sweetheart, you're a precious gift to this family."

She shrugs and says, "You have to say that. But I want Sly to be happy, and what if I'm the reason he decides not to marry her?"

"Look at me," I urge, lifting her chin with my finger. "Never forget, you are the icing on the cake." We smile at the memory of Daddy saying those words to her.

As Maggie finishes polishing her nails, our conversation plays through my mind. My 12-year-old sister is worried she'll cost Sly her happiness. That's a weight too heavy for her to carry, and it's another thing Anthony Avery must answer for.

8

Saturday, October 13
10:30 a.m.

"Hurry, Grace. I promised Cole we'd be at the ranch by 10:45 a.m. The party starts at 11:00." I glance over at Grace as she buckles her seatbelt, and, for the first time, I notice her shiny belt buckle.

"I didn't know you were on the rodeo circuit," I tease.

Grace glances down at the silver buckle at her waist. "Oh, this old thing?" She laughs self-consciously. "Wait, is it too much? Dad loaned it to me for authenticity."

"It's great," I reassure her. "I forgot your dad used to rodeo in his college days. He must have been pretty talented to earn a buckle."

Grace reverently touches the metal. "Yes, although he only did it long enough to make extra tuition money. I'm glad he stopped before he got hurt."

"You look like a genuine cowgirl. The girls will love it."

I pull my braid over my shoulder and waggle the bandana ribbon attached to the end. "This is my costume." I grin. "I'll be doing grunt work in the stables while you're corralling the guests."

"This will be fun," Grace says. "I'll thank Cole for recommending me to Ben."

"Don't thank him yet," I laugh. "I'm positive you'll earn every dollar of your paycheck today. Cole texted me before I left the house and said he saw the guest list. Our favorite twins are on it."

"Janey and Joey?" Grace frowns as she considers this news. "I mean, I love them, of course, but aren't they a little young for a horse-riding birthday celebration? The birthday girl is eight. Her name is Corrie Whitmer, right?"

"Yes," I answer both questions. "But they must be friends because they are two of the twelve guests."

"Don't worry," I say as Grace's eyes widen at the size of the group. "It's a kid's birthday party. What could go wrong?"

As it turns out, a lot can go wrong.

Our first clue is when Mrs. Ellison meets us at the stables when I park Sly's Honda.

"Oh, I'm so relieved to see you." She opens Grace's door and all but yanks her from the car.

"Jennifer forgot to pick up the cake, of all things. She's in a panic, so I promised I'd run back into town and get it." Sandra Ellison waves towards a frazzled-looking woman standing under the covered shelter, surrounded by restless children. One girl is wearing a pink cowboy hat with a Birthday Girl tiara attached to the front. Jennifer and Corrie Whitmer wear similar expressions of sorrow, probably caused by the missing cake.

Mrs. Ellison grabs our hands and tugs us toward the celebration. "I told Jennifer how wonderful you and Jess are with the twins. I'm positive you'll be able to help her run the party until I return with the cake."

She presents us to the group like we're the finale to a magic trick, and I'm sure she mutters, "Ta-Da!"

All eyes turn to us, and I suddenly remember what Ben hired me to do. This isn't it. "Um, I should help Cole with the ponies," I mutter.

At the word ponies, the children hop up and down, yelling, "Ponies! We want to ride the ponies, now!"

Then Cole is beside me, raising his hand in a "Stop" gesture. They stop.

"The ponies are as excited as you are," Cole says. "But they aren't quite ready yet." He glances at Mrs. Whitmer. "Ben said you had a few games planned first, right?"

"Yes." Mrs. Whitmer takes a deep breath drawing in some calm as well as oxygen. "Grace can help with the games while Sandra picks up the cake. Afterward, we can ride the ponies."

There are a few grumbles, but Grace corrals the guests to the shelter, where several games are waiting.

"Whew, thanks for the rescue." I walk with Cole toward the stables, where the two ponies live. I hear Mrs. Ellison's SUV engine start and watch the dust swirl behind her.

"Crisis averted," Cole says. "How about you saddle Pebbles, and I'll take care of Rocky?"

I step to the stall where the sturdy pony stands. As my finger glides over her velvety nose, I murmur, "Hello, sweet girl. Are you excited about the party?"

In the next stall, Rocky snorts as Cole swings the saddle onto his back. Rocky complains a little when the saddle first goes on, but he's always a perfect gentleman with the kids.

Across the yard, the children are yelling as they play a rousing game of Red Rover.

Through the open door, I spot Joey standing apart from the others. He's wearing jeans and a white denim shirt. His mom has tied a bandana at his neck. It's red with black lassos outlined in sparkling gold.

He lifts his trusty bow and notches an arrow, as I showed him. He pulls it back as far as his thin arms can manage and lets it fly. The arrow sails straight into a little girl's hair, and she spins, frowning at Joey.

He gives a gap-toothed grin. "Sowwy," he says as he runs to collect his single arrow.

The girl, who must be about nine, appears charmed by his lisp. "That's okay," she smiles as she returns to the game.

I grin and turn back to see Cole leading Rocky from his stall.

"C'mon Pebbles." I address the pretty pony and unlatch her gate. "Showtime."

We lead the ponies through the back door so we don't distract the kids from their game.

"Could you tell Mrs. Whitmer we're ready?" Cole takes Pebble's lead from my grip and ties the ponies to the fence.

I follow the sounds of shouts and laughter and approach Mrs. Whitmer. She's using her pink bandana to dab at the beads of sweat dotting her temple. She's drooping already, and the fun has barely started. I remind myself that motherhood is not for wimps.

"We're ready," I whisper, but the girls catch on immediately.

"Pony rides!" The chant starts again, and I hold up my hand as Cole did earlier, hoping to stop the noise. No such luck. In fact, they become louder. How did he do that?

As suddenly as the hollering began, it stops. Maybe I do have silencing skills. Then I sense Cole is standing behind me. Of course.

"Okay, guys, here are the rules," Cole says. "Rocky and Pebbles are gentle ponies, but they can get spooked. You'll need to stay calm as we move by the corral. Benches are sitting outside the paddock, so take your seat, and you'll each have a turn. Jess and I will lead your ponies. I understand some of you have ridden before, but today everyone rides with a lead."

The guests nod, eagerly agreeing to anything that will get them on a pony.

Grace suggests, "Let's make a line, starting with the birthday girl."

Corrie giggles and skips to stand by Grace, who forms the line according to age, starting with the oldest first. Hopefully, when the younger kids are ready for their turn, they'll have calmed down a little.

I follow Cole to the paddock and see Joey standing at the end of the line. He's wiggling a little, and I hope when he sits on his pony, he's shaken the willies out, as my Grandmother Thomas used to say.

The line snakes around the corner, but when the kids spot the ponies, their control shatters.

They nearly trample Grace as they break ranks and race to where Cole has tied Rocky and Pebbles.

"Oh, they're so pretty." Several girls reach out, petting the ponies, and Rocky jerks his head away, snorting. Cole's long strides take him to the fence, and he reaches up to calm Rocky. I herd the girls to the benches, and Grace gives us an apologetic grimace.

"Sorry."

"No problem," Cole assures her. "I'll give them a few minutes to settle down."

I'm not sure if he's referring to the girls or the ponies, but I figure it's a plan either way.

Cole spends the next few minutes giving basic instructions. "Once I put you in the saddle, you'll take the reins in your hands," he says, holding up the reins. "Don't jerk on them because that will hurt the pony's mouth. Then hold on to the pommel and grip your knees against the pony's side to steady yourself. I'll lead you around the arena two times.

When you finish your ride, please wait for me to take you off the pony. Don't climb down on your own. Everyone understand?"

A chorus of 'yeses' sounds, and soon we have our first riders in the saddle. Corrie grasps the pommel so tightly her tiny knuckles are white, and I give her an encouraging smile.

"You're doing great, honey. I think Pebbles likes you." She

relaxes her grip slightly, and by the time we make the first circuit around the paddock, she's grinning.

As I lead the next two girls to where Cole waits, I notice Grace and Mrs. Whitmer in deep conversation.

"Wait," I say to Cole, hurrying to where they are standing by the fence.

"Is something wrong?" I ask.

"Joey's not back from the bathroom yet," Grace responds, a frown creasing her forehead.

"How long has he been gone?"

"He needed to use the restroom," Mrs. Whitmer answers. "He showed me the bathroom by the stable, and I said, yes, but hurry to join us."

Her French braid has unraveled, and damp tendrils stick to her face. It's a good thing Corrie only has one birthday party per year.

"I'll get him," Grace offers, and she sprints off toward the stable.

"I'm sure he's fine," I reassure Mrs. Whitmer. "He probably stopped to shoot his bow and arrow some more."

She nods uncertainly, and I hurry over to help Cole with the next rides.

We're finishing our second trip around the arena when I see Grace sprinting across the yard to join Mrs. Whitmer. There's no sign of Joey.

"Jess?" There's a question in Cole's voice as he watches Grace's mad dash.

"Let's give the ponies a rest," I say. I don't want to alarm the two inexperienced riders who might react in fear and spook the ponies.

Cole nods, and soon he lifts the riders from the saddles and ties the ponies' leads to the fence.

Groans erupt from the group as they realize we've stopped the rides.

"They need a breather," Cole tells them, following me to where Grace and Mrs. Whitmer stand.

"Problem?" he asks.

"I've searched everywhere." Tears form in Grace's eyes. "Joey is gone."

9

Saturday, October 13
11:00 a.m.

"I'll get Ben." Cole sprints toward the stables.

"Where did you check?" I ask. Grace has visited the ranch twice, and I'm sure she doesn't know all the hiding places a little boy could find. Joey. My heart skips a beat. Our Joey.

"I checked the bathroom, shelter, and the stable. I didn't want to spook the horses by yelling his name, but I walked around and peeked in each stall. He's not there." Grace's voice shakes.

"Mommy?" Corrie pulls on Mrs. Whitmer's arm. "Can we still ride the ponies?"

"In a few minutes, honey. Cole had to ask Mr. Hadley a question, and soon we'll finish the pony rides. Grace, can you think of a game to play while we wait?"

Grace tries to smile at Corrie, but it comes out more like a grimace. "Sure. Let's play Duck, Duck, Goose." Grace leads the birthday girl away but glances over her shoulder, obviously wishing she could stay. Her face is pale, and her red-blonde hair highlights the freckles across her cheeks.

"Yoo-hoo." Mrs. Ellison waves at us from the shelter. "Cake has arrived," she sings out.

Mrs. Whitmer catches her breath. "How can I tell her?" By now, tears are streaking down her cheeks, and I gently touch her arm.

"I'm sure he's fine," I try to reassure us both. "Let's go talk to her together. Then I'll help Cole and Ben with the search."

She nods, stumbling a little as she follows me to the shelter.

Mrs. Ellison is busy setting out plates and napkins. Her back is to us, and she calls out, "Sorry it took so long. Unfortunately, the bakery was running late. They did an amazing job, though."

She steps back to reveal a cake in the shape of a white pony. Swirls of pink and lavender frosting decorate the mane.

Mrs. Whitmer gives a choked sob, and Mrs. Ellison turns abruptly, frowning in concern.

I step forward to say, "Mrs. Ellison, we can have the cake as soon as we locate Joey. He's exploring, and Cole and Mr. Hadley are looking for him." I try to avoid words like lost, missing, and search, but Mrs. Ellison is a smart lady.

"Joey is missing?" Her voice carries a squeak of fear.

"No," I assure her. "He asked to use the bathroom. He probably decided to wander around the ranch a while before he returned to the party. I'm sure they'll locate him any minute."

"How long?" Mrs. Ellison asks tersely.

Mrs. Whitmer answers through tears. "Twenty minutes. Sandra, I'm so sorry,"

Mrs. Ellison draws in a quick breath. "Twenty minutes is a long time." She chokes the words, and I can see panic rising.

"I'm so sorry." Mrs. Whitmer repeats, crying harder now. "The bathroom was around the corner, and it never occurred to me he wouldn't come straight back."

I want to ask, "Have you *met* Joey?" but restrain myself, remembering that not everyone understands I use sarcasm to cope with stress.

Mrs. Ellison wraps her arms around her sobbing friend. "My

Joey is an explorer," "she says but her voice waivers. "I'm sure he wandered off to look at the horses, and they'll find him any minute."

Those last words sound more like a prayer.

"Wait, where is Janey?" Mrs. Ellison swivels around in panic, and I hurry to explain that Janey and the other girls are at the paddock with Grace. I say a quick prayer for Grace and regret leaving her alone to deal with eleven little girls on her own.

As we leave the shelter, the two moms walk arm in arm, comforting each other even as they try to act normal and not frighten the other children.

"Jess." Cole's voice stops me, and I watch him walk toward me, followed by Ben Hadley, Keith Robertson, and ... Amy Sinclair.

'Please, will this nightmare never end?' I push away the selfish thought. I appreciate any help. Even Amy's.

"Did you find Joey?" I ask.

"No." Cole's gray eyes reflect his concern. "We've checked all the buildings, and there's no sign of him."

I shake my head in disbelief. "But where is there to go? You checked the main house?"

"I did," Amy says. Concern pinches her brows.

"As to where he could go ..." Ben nods toward the thick woods at the edge of the property.

"No way," I insist.

Joey is barely five years old, and I can't consider that possibility. "He'd be more interested in looking at the horses than wandering in the woods." The panic in my voice suggests I'm trying to persuade myself as much as Ben.

"I called SARS," Ben says the words that make this nightmare all too real. SARS Search and Rescue teams look for missing people. Missing people like Joey.

"Normally, I might give it more time, but because of his age and ... other concerns, I thought I should get them here pronto," Ben adds.

"Other concerns?" I ask.

Cole and Ben exchange a glance, and Cole answers. "Tom Gleason from the ranch north of here called Ben a while ago. A cougar attacked one of his horses this morning. Tom shot his rifle but missed, and he wanted Ben to know it was moving into the woods between their two ranches."

I glance again at the woods. The woods where Joey might be, and my knees buckle.

"Jess," Cole steadies me.

"Mrs. Ellison," I breathe. "We have to tell her."

"I'm headed there now," Ben explains. "I was already planning to move the group into the main house after Tom called me. So, let's get that done, then we'll organize the search."

My wobbly legs carry me to the yard, where Mrs. Ellison, Mrs. Whitmer, and Grace are coaxing the girls into another game.

"I'm hungry," one girl complains.

"When can I open presents?" Corrie asks.

Mrs. Ellison sees us approaching and hurries to Ben. "Mr. Hadley, did you find my son?"

"Not yet, ma'am," Ben says, "but we're focusing everyone on the job. Now, I think it would be best to move the party into the main house. That way, the searchers won't alarm the girls."

Mrs. Ellison nods, and soon we're all herding the girls into Ben's sprawling ranch house. His wife, Edith, greets us at the door and, with a somewhat forced cheerfulness, says, "Well, isn't this fun. I love a birthday party."

Edith, Grace, and Mrs. Whitmer set up the hot dogs, chips, and drinks in the expansive dining room, placing the pony cake in the middle of the table. Distracted, the girls stop complaining about the lost pony rides. Mrs. Whitmer distributes food with promises of gifts and cake to follow.

I see Cole leave to stable Pebbles and Rocky, and I'm irritated when Amy follows him.

I push down my jealousy, knowing this is not the moment. A

tiny hand slips into mine, and I glance down, meeting Janey's bright blue eyes.

"Where's Joey?" she asks.

I'm not sure what Mrs. Ellison told Janey about her missing twin. I certainly don't want to lie, but I shouldn't tell her the truth, either. A wave of relief sweeps through me when Mrs. Ellison hurries over.

"Janey, remember, I told you Joey is on an adventure. He'll be back soon. Let's join the other girls and have some lunch." Mrs. Ellison turns toward the dining room, but Janey doesn't move.

"Joey is scared," Janey says, and Mrs. Ellison and I exchange startled looks.

"Baby, do you know where Joey is?" Mrs. Ellison kneels to study her daughter.

"No." Janey shakes her head, causing her curly ponytails to whip around. The sight of her bright pink, gingham ribbons causes tears to sting my eyes. Only a few hours earlier, Mrs. Ellison had tied those bows, likely laughing about all the fun they'd have today. Those pink ribbons are a cruel reminder of how quickly circumstances can change.

"He's scared," Janey repeats and starts to cry. She doesn't make any noise. Instead, she lets the huge tears roll down her face.

"Sweetheart." Mrs. Ellison gathers Janey into her arms and carries her to the attached family room. They settle into an oversized chair, and I hear her say, "Janey, let's pray and ask God to help Joey not be scared, okay? Your daddy is on his way here, and he's bringing Grandma with him so she can take you home." Mrs. Ellison rubs soothing circles on Janey's back, and I turn away, giving them privacy.

From the front porch, I see several SUVs pulling into the parking area near the stables. A glance toward the paddock shows Cole and Amy leading the ponies to the stables, and I head in that direction too. It's time to join the search for Joey.

10

Saturday, October 13
12:30 p.m.

"I'm sorry, Jess, you can't go." Nick is pulling equipment from his vehicle, and at first, I'm positive I misunderstood him.

Nick is one of the SARS leaders, and it relieved me when I saw him leading this team. Now I'm not so confident.

"Nick, I realize you think I'm kind of a loose cannon," I say, but he interrupts me.

"True, but that's not why you can't participate." Nick crosses the yard toward the area where the searchers wait, some on four-wheelers but most sitting horseback. I recognize several local ranchers, and I'm glad there's such a sizable turnout. They'll find Joey soon.

"You're too young." Nick launches himself into Fury's saddle.

Pointing to Cole and Amy, who are riding Chieftain and Damsel, I say, "I'm not either." I immediately regret that I sound like I'm ten. "I'll be seventeen next month."

"You are still sixteen, Jess. SARS has a strict requirement that a searcher must be eighteen, which Cole and Amy meet." His tense face relaxes a little. "I understand you're worried, but

I'm positive there's something you can do here to help. We may need food, so you and Grace can take Cole's truck and pick up the sandwiches Walmart is providing for the searchers."

Touching the keys in my pocket, I now understand why Cole handed them to me. He already knew I wouldn't be able to ride with him and Amy.

I glance up to catch Amy regarding me, and I swear her mouth twists on a slight smirk. I raise my head and walk toward where Cole sits astride Chieftain.

"Be careful," I say and turn aside before he can respond.

The living room is quiet when I enter. Over the past hour, Edith and Grace fed the party guests, then called their parents. Annabelle Johnson's mom offered to take several girls to her house so more parents could join the search.

Finally, Mr. Ellison and Grandma Martin arrive. In the kitchen, they're encouraging Janey to go home with her grandmother. But when Janey spots me, she launches herself into my arms. I gather her up, and her silent tears break my heart.

I carry her to Grandma Martin's sedan and settle her into the car seat. Then her tiny voice whispers in my ear, "They're looking in the wrong place."

Startled, I ask, "What do you mean?"

But crying has exhausted Janey. She turns her head into the cushioned headrest and is asleep.

I return to the house and hear Ben telling Mr. and Mrs. Ellison a rancher spotted the cougar in the area. Mrs. Ellison's cry will haunt my dreams. Mr. Ellison comforts his wife, but it's obvious he wants to join the search for his son. He clutches Joey's pajama top, which he brought in case they need the search dogs. The concern with dogs is they might scare Joey into hiding, but they're available if necessary.

Edith Hadley wraps her arms around Mrs. Ellison. "Here, Sandra, let's sit, and you can tell me about Joey. Then, maybe between us, we can think where he might go."

I want to mention we've searched every nook and cranny of

the ranch, but then I understand Edith is making Mrs. Ellison feel useful. Pain tingles as I clench my fists, digging my nails into my palms. I have to *do* something.

The vibration of horse's hooves draws my attention, and from the porch, I watch the searchers ride away. No one rides alone, and at least one person in each group carries a rifle in case they encounter the cougar.

My heart hurts when I think of Joey's little boy bravery as he practiced using his bow and arrow.

"I'm gonna' twack the tiger." My nose burns with unshed tears, and I impatiently shake my head. Crying won't help find Joey.

Janey's words echo in my mind. *"They're looking in the wrong place."* I've heard twins can sometimes have a connection that runs so deep they feel each other's emotions. The searchers are in the woods. What if Joey is still here? Hurt? Or hiding because he's scared he's in trouble?

I hurry to the stables. Joey is so tiny; he could be curled in a corner somewhere, sound asleep.

When Nick was organizing the searchers, he explained it isn't unusual for young children to become lost and hide if they are frightened. Sometimes they even find a warm spot and fall asleep. Warm. Although the day is a pleasant 60 degrees, the evening chill will remind us it's October. Joey is wearing a light denim shirt and jeans, but that won't be enough if he's still missing by tonight.

I search through the stable, knowing I'll find nothing. Some ranchers brought their own horses, but Ben supplied the others, and now the stable is quiet. A snort startles me. The end stall belongs to Daisy, a sweet mare I've ridden a few times.

"Hey, girl," I pat her velvet nose. "What's wrong? Are you too young too?"

Daisy snorts again and shakes her head, as if nodding in agreement.

"Yeah," I sigh. "I know the feeling."

I move away, seeing Daisy's saddle lying over the wall. A

thought pops into my mind, and I fight to dismiss it. No. Nick said to stay here. I walk away, then spin back.

"They're looking in the wrong place."

I tug on the saddle with my typical impulsiveness. In minutes Daisy and I are racing across the stable yard toward the woods. I'll help search, and when we find Joey, I'll return Daisy without Nick ever knowing.

I falter when I realize Cole might know, though. Cole is a horse ninja—he'll recognize someone rode Daisy, even if I get her back, watered, and brushed. He'll know.

My recklessness is an ongoing problem between Cole and me. I've occasionally—okay, often—made rash decisions that put me in danger, and Cole calls me on it every time. But this is different, I assure myself. Cole will understand. This is Joey. The nagging picture I have of Cole and Amy riding together does not influence my decision. Not at all.

In the distance, the voices of the searchers call, "Joey! Joey Ellison." Most of them are in the woods that border the ranch property. That makes sense, of course. Joey is only five, and his little legs couldn't have carried him very far.

I head to a part of the woods farther away, assuming Nick didn't assign anyone there. I realize it's a long shot, but Joey disappeared three hours ago. He might have come in this direction.

As we enter the woods, the air is cooler, and again, I think of Joey's tiny, shivering body. I can't ride fast because there's no trail, and we have to pick our way through the trees. I call Joey's name and listen, hoping to hear an answering cry.

For a minute, I imagine finding Joey and wrapping him in the blanket I borrowed from Daisy's stall. Yes, it's rough and, well, horsey, but it's also warm, and that's what matters.

The musty smell of algae reminds me Grasshopper Creek runs alongside the ranch property, and now I have another fear. What if Joey slipped and fell into the water?

I nudge Daisy toward the creek and take deep breaths,

attempting to stay calm. Usually, I love the piney smell of the woods, but now it reminds me that Joey is in a strange place and possibly in danger.

We enter a clearing where I can scan the banks of the creek. Across from us, I see a startled deer raise its head and then lope away. Another concern grips me as I realize wild animals come to this creek to drink.

There's no sign of a cold, scared little boy, so Daisy and I head back into the woods. But we've only gone a few yards when Daisy shakes her head and snorts in obvious distress. I tug on the reins and pull up. "What is it, girl?"

Daisy settles, and I pat her neck. "Easy. I realize these woods are spooky, but we'll find Joey soon, and I'll take you back for a yummy meal of mash."

That reassures her, and she moves again, then stops so abruptly she nearly tosses me over her head.

The back of my neck tickles with awareness of ... what? Was there a noise? Did Joey call out?

Daisy and I spot the cougar at the same time. I realize this because I see Daisy's eyes roll in fear even as I scream.

This is the first time I've seen him in daylight, and I'm stunned. True North said Outlaw is close to seven feet and likely weighs over 200 pounds. What he didn't describe is his terrifying beauty. Sleek and powerful, his coat is a reddish tan, and he has a white muzzle. His tail is easily three feet long, tipped in black. Outlaw stands about 30 feet from us, watching with that steely green one-eyed stare.

Daisy spooks, lunging sideways, and I nearly topple over. Panic pools in my stomach, and I fight to stay upright. If I fall, Daisy will bolt, and I'll be cougar food.

Outlaw growls, and now Daisy rears. I slip, and I grapple for the pommel. Reins are secondary; Daisy will pull them right through my fingers when she runs. I lay forward across the saddle and wrap my knees around Daisy's girth. I focus on staying upright and almost forget about Outlaw.

But he reminds me when he gives a piercing screech. Birds fly out of the trees, startled from their safe perch.

Daisy rears again, and I'm jolted so hard against her back I bite my tongue. Blood fills my mouth as Outlaw and I stare at each other, and I say the only thing that comes to my mind.

"God, help me."

Outlaw tips his head at an angle as if struggling to translate my words. I repeat them. Louder.

"God, help me."

The cougar growls and paces, his impossibly long tail twitching.

From the corner of my eye, I catch a glittery flash and peer closer at a leaf-covered fallen log. Glitter flashes again, and now I recognize the source. Joey's bandana with the black lassos edged in gold. My heart races as his small, terrified face stares up at me.

Joey!

As if Outlaw senses my thoughts, he gives a low growl and stalks toward Joey.

I scan the area in panic, trying to find something, anything, to draw Outlaw's attention. Remembering True's advice, I stand in the stirrups, wildly waving my arms above my head.

"Hey, cougar! Yeah, you, Outlaw. Get out of here!"

Beneath me, Daisy lurches sideways, and I can barely stay on her back. Outlaw, unimpressed by my shouting, continues toward Joey, who is sobbing now. I sit in the saddle and tug the reins, urging Daisy forward. But the poor horse is out of her mind with fear, and she balks, sidestepping to avoid the cougar.

Outlaw is pacing in front of Joey, purring as if he's enjoying his game of terror. My heart is pounding so hard I can barely breathe.

Then I see the moment Joey decides to run.

"Joey, no!" I wail.

Joey stands, and Outlaw bunches his powerful legs to prepare for the leap as he gives a terrifying wail.

"Help us, God!" The strangled words feel torn from my throat, even as Outlaw hurtles through the air.

Time stops. I see Joey's tear-streaked face, his mouth opened in horror. Outlaw is impossibly long, suspended in midair, scant yards from the little boy.

"Help us, God," I sob.

Then Outlaw is flat on the ground as if he hit an invisible barrier. He lays, stunned for a second, then stands and emits a sharp yip. Finally, he takes a step backward, rolling his shoulders down in a defensive move opposite from his earlier aggression.

With a whine, he backs away, giving me a glare that promises, "Another time."

I sincerely hope not.

Outlaw disappears, leaving an unexpected stillness behind.

"Jess. You found me." Joey's words are a strange echo from my dream a few days earlier.

I'm off Daisy's back in a second, falling to the rough ground to hold Joey. "Sweetheart, are you okay?"

His warm tears trickle onto my neck. "I was twacking the tiger," he sobs. "But he was so big I got scared."

"Me too," I agree.

"I was hiding, but he saw me, and you came and made him run away." The words tumble out in a breathless rush.

I want to explain that I didn't do anything, but I still can't process what I saw.

"We're all safe now," I assure him. "Daisy and I will take you home."

I take Joey's hand and wrap the blanket around his shoulders, then lift him to sit on Daisy's neck. I swing into the saddle, catching Joey as he slides. He just escaped a cougar; I don't want to break him now.

I wish I could kick Daisy into a gallop, but the trees are thick here, so our progress is slow. Joey snuggles against me, and I'm relieved he's stopped shaking.

The back of my neck prickles and I'm sure if I check, I'll see the cat's one-eyed stare following our escape. But I focus on the path, and the words of a scripture fill my mind, "The God of Israel will be your rear guard."

I sit up straighter in the saddle and let Daisy lead us home.

My teeth are chattering by the time we emerge from the woods. I'm not sure if I'm in shock or cold, but either way, I tighten my jaw to keep from biting my tongue again. The metallic taste of blood is making me nauseous.

SARS routinely dispatches an ambulance for a search, and now one waits in the driveway. My pulse quickens as I glance over the pasture where several riders are emerging from the woods.

One rider notices me and breaks away from the others, galloping toward us.

I want to gallop too, but our adventure has exhausted poor Daisy. I shift in the saddle as Cole and Chieftain cross the wide pasture and pull up, facing me.

Before Cole can speak, Joey lifts his chin. "Hi, Cole. Jess scared that mean tiger away."

I can read the variety of emotions playing over Cole's face. First, relief Joey is safe, then alarm at the word tiger, followed by anger that I was even there. And somewhere mixed in, I catch a glimmer of pride. Poor Cole. I'm sure I'm a very confusing girlfriend.

Within minutes, we enter the stable yard, and Joey tumbles into Mr. Ellison's waiting arms. Mrs. Ellison races from the house to join the reunion.

"We'll take excellent care of him." The EMT approaches with a gurney and assures the Ellisons.

"Please, can I go with you?" Mrs. Ellison pleads.

The EMT nods. "One parent can go."

They lift Joey into the back of the ambulance, his precious bow and arrow still tight in his grasp. I turn aside, my own emotions threatening to overwhelm me. Suddenly Cole's arms are around me, and I break. All the terror from the past few hours releases as I cry into his denim jacket.

Someone, Keith probably, takes Daisy's reins and leads her to the stable. "Please take care of her," I call out. "She's had a rough ride."

"What about you?" Cole turns me to face him and frowns as he wipes his hand over my mouth. "You're bleeding."

"I bit my tongue."

"I'm biting mine, too." Nick stands beside us. "There's no time now, but later we'll talk about this." He moves aside, but I stop him with a hand on his arm.

Taking a deep breath, I say, "Nick, the cougar is in the woods." I point in the direction that Daisy and I had ridden. "I saw him there only thirty minutes ago."

I try to read the emotions that play over Nick's face and decide I prefer not to know.

He gives a curt nod and goes to consult with the team.

Cole's arms tighten on me, and in his gray eyes, I witness the return of fear and fury.

"Cole, I ..." but an abrupt shake of his head stops me.

"Are you hurt, other than your tongue?"

I shake my head, and I'm released. "I'll go check on Daisy," he says and walks away.

I'm startled when a voice whispers in my ear, "You never learn, do you?" Then Amy Sinclair follows Cole into the stable, and I can hear my heart break.

11

My Tweety alarm chirps, and I barely resist the impulse to throw it across the room. Instead, I pull the pillow over my head and try muffling the annoying sound. A moment later, the noise mysteriously stops. A thump lands on top of the cushion, and I take a peek. Sly is standing over me.

"Wake up."

"No."

"Yes." She tugs on the pillow.

"No." I grip it tighter, curling into a tight ball of misery.

It's quiet for a moment, and I lift the pillow. Sly is still standing beside the bed, watching me with concern. That expression is my undoing. I prefer her anger over compassion.

"Hey." Sly sits on the edge of the bed. "You can't hide there all day, you know."

"Wanna bet?" I muffle my reply under the pillow.

She sighs. "One of your best traits is when you mess up, you accept responsibility. Hiding is not your style."

"Maybe I got a makeover."

"Doubtful. At your core, you're courageous, Jess. The same

courage that helped you face Outlaw yesterday is the courage that will get you up and moving today. No matter what comes."

"Cole hates me." I wince at the whine in my voice.

Sly laughs. Actually laughs! "Of course, he doesn't hate you. In fact, I think he loves you—that's why he's so mad. We're all relieved you found Joey, but every time I think of you riding off alone and facing Outlaw, I want to shake you. What you did was reckless and dangerous. Cole has a reason to be angry."

I lift the pillow and look up at her.

"Isn't this supposed to be a pep talk?" I grumble.

"It is. I'm encouraging you to own your mistakes and apologize to Cole for scaring him. You did that for me last night. It was good practice."

"It's different with you. You're my sister, and I know you'll always love me no matter how mad you are at me. I'm not so sure about Cole."

"I understand. But that's why you have to talk to him. Those tough conversations are the most important when you're building a relationship."

Sly stands. "There's enough time to get ready and join us for church. I'll have a warm blueberry muffin and a mug of coffee ready for you to take in the car." She leaves without waiting for my response.

I'd like to pull the pillow back and hide in bed all day, but that isn't who I am. I meet my problems head-on.

My emotions are so jumbled. First, of course, I'm thrilled Joey is safe. When the Ellisons called to thank me for finding him, I was proud and a little embarrassed. But I also feel guilty for scaring Cole and Nick, even though the outcome was positive. Stupid, confusing emotions!

Twenty minutes later, I'm wolfing down my breakfast as Sly drives us to church. Maggie is quiet, and I make a mental note to talk to her later today. Although she wasn't aware of what happened until after the fact, I'm sure she's unsettled by knowing I faced Outlaw again. I know I am.

Worship is starting when we arrive, so we slip into a back row, and I slump in my chair, trying to be invisible. Even so, several people stop to hug me or pat my shoulder, and if I hear the word *hero* one more time, I'll scream.

I plan to leave after Pastor Jeff says the last amen. I'm hoping to avoid conversations, questions, and plans for a parade in my honor.

Grace and her family sit three rows ahead of us, and Grace glances back, waving to attract my attention. I give a halfhearted wiggle of my fingers, and she smiles. At least Grace forgave me. Of course, she had her chance to tell me off last night, so she had a head start on the process.

Last night I tried to describe when Outlaw seemed to hit an invisible shield.

"One minute, Outlaw was sailing through the air, and the next, he was flat on the ground."

"Maybe it was an angel," Sly suggests.

"Probably Joey's," Grace says. "I think all of Jess's angels asked for a transfer."

Every time I think of how God protected Joey, Daisy, and me, I'm in awe. I shiver when I think about Joey repeating the words in my dream. *"You found me."*

I'm eager to tell Cole the story. Too bad he's mad at me. I haven't spoken to him since he stomped away yesterday, Amy on his heels. Who knows what she said about me? Nothing good, I'm sure.

The service ends, and I forget my plan to escape when I spot Cole. He's talking to a beautiful young woman I've never seen before today. I turn to leave, nearly knocking Grace over.

"Oomph." Grace grunts and staggers.

"Sorry." I stop long enough to steady her, then turn and hurtle toward the exit. I have to leave. Now.

"Wait!" Grace races to catch me, teetering a little on the wedge heels she's wearing. "Slow down."

I yank open the car door and throw myself into the back seat.

Grace slides in beside me. "What's wrong?"

"Nothing." I swipe furiously at the stupid tears stinging my eyes.

"Nope, that's not how this works. This is me. Grace. You can try the 'nothing' answer with other people, but not me." Grace leans around to study my face. "Jess, please tell me what's wrong."

"I wanted to tell Cole how sorry I am that I took Daisy and almost got eaten by the cougar. But he was talking to some strange, gorgeous girl."

"She's gorgeous, but she is not some strange girl."

"Whaaa—"

I try to retort before Grace continues, "Her name is Amanda Jackson, and she recently became engaged to Pastor Jeff's son, Matt. They drove down from Helena to celebrate with his family this weekend."

"How do you know these things?" I ask in surprise.

"I have my sources," Grace says breezily. "The point is, she's taken, and he isn't flirting with her. I doubt if Cole even knows how to flirt."

Slightly mollified, I give a brief smile. "He does."

"Well, you should know. And speaking of Cole, here he comes."

I swivel to watch Cole cross the parking lot in long, determined strides.

"Hmm," observes Grace. "He seems ... pensive."

I frown at her, and she shrugs. "What? Pensive is my word of the day. And it fits."

Grace reaches for the door handle, and I grab her arm. "Wait, where are you going?" I try to disguise the panic in my voice.

"To lunch with Kellen. He's not pensive. He's tranquil." She beams. "That's tomorrow's word."

I shake my head, momentarily distracted. "Only you would study ahead on your word of the day calendar."

"I like to be prepared." She opens the door and climbs out of the car.

I'm startled by a tap at my window, where Cole stands watching me. Pensively.

I take a deep breath and roll down the window.

"Yes?" I try for a bright smile, but I'm pretty sure it's more like a grimace.

"Do you have plans for lunch?"

I consider telling him I'm busy this afternoon, dusting the garage. But his expression shows he's not in the mood for jokes. "No," I say.

"Let's take some burgers up to the Rock. I already cleared it with Sly."

I follow Cole to his truck, and sooner than I want, we're driving up the mountain, burgers and two drinks balanced between us. Other than asking what I want to eat, Cole hasn't said a word. This should be fun. Not.

We take the short path to the big flat rock, which offers a fantastic view of the Pioneer Mountains. Above the tree line, the peaks tickle a parade of clouds. The day is cool but sunny, and Cole spreads out a blanket he took from his truck bed. It smells a little like hay, but that's okay, and I settle down to eat my lunch.

I nibble on the edge of my burger, nerves stealing my appetite. After a few bites, I give up and wrap the sandwich, but Cole stops me.

"Are you going to eat that?"

Wordlessly I hand him the burger, and within seconds he devours it. I shake my head in amazement. Guys. Nothing spoils their appetite.

Cole gathers up our trash and stashes it in the truck for later disposal. Then he's sitting beside me again, and the waiting is over.

"Let's talk," he says. "Tell me what happened."

His request surprises me. I expected anger, but he leans forward as if he doesn't want to miss a word.

I draw in a deep breath and explain. "I was heartbroken, thinking about Joey, lost in the woods. He's so little I knew it must terrify him. I felt helpless wandering around the ranch, not able to help with the search."

Cole's watchful expression urges me to continue.

"Janey said the searchers were looking in the wrong place. At first, I thought she meant Joey was still near the stables, so I started there, even though we searched it a dozen times. When I saw Daisy in her stall, I guess I reacted. I figured a quick ride to check wouldn't hurt anything.

Since there's no cell service in the woods, I couldn't tell you what Janey said. Trust me, meeting the cougar was *not* in my plans."

Cole's jaw tightens. "I'm sure," is all he says. "Go on."

I describe meeting Outlaw near the creek and spotting Joey under the leaves. When I get to the part where Outlaw hit something, Cole's eyes widen.

"God saved our lives. There's no other explanation." I shiver, remembering the strange expression in the animal's eye.

Cole sits quietly for a minute, staring out at the mountains. "You're right," he says. "Only God could do that."

He turns to face me, his gray eyes serious. "But you can't keep taking risks, assuming God will protect you. You have a responsibility to make wise decisions."

"I know," I agree. "I'm thankful God protected me in the past few months, first with Robert Sinclair and then Outlaw. But I don't plan to take advantage of His faithfulness by being reckless."

Cole studies me for a minute. "Did Amy Sinclair have anything to do with your decision to ride Daisy?"

A flush warms my cheeks. I desperately want to turn away but force myself to hold his gaze.

"A little, I guess. I'd like to think I did it only for Joey, but when you two rode away together ..." My voice trails off at Cole's tense expression.

"We weren't riding together. We had different partners by the time we got to the woods." He sighs and reaches for my hand. "Jess, I need you to listen to me. I'm not interested in Amy Sinclair. I'll never be interested in Amy Sinclair.

"I don't like to say anything bad about her, so I'll only tell you this once. Amy is everything I don't like in a girl. She's arrogant, spoiled, and sometimes, just plain mean."

For a minute, Cole stares at the mountains, and I wait, sensing what comes next is important. When he faces me again, I'm surprised to see a flush creep up his neck and under the stubble on his cheeks.

"Jess, do you trust me?"

While the hurt in his gray eyes creates a tiny crack in my heart, his vulnerable question fractures it. I nod, unable to speak.

"Thank you," he says.

And I realize it's the truth. Cole's never given me any reason not to trust him.

"When you're jealous of Amy, I feel like you doubt me, not her. Do you understand?"

Hot tears sting my eyes, and I lay my head over to nudge his shoulder. "I'm so sorry," I say. "I hadn't thought of it that way. She's just so ..." I try to think of the correct word, wishing I had Grace's word-a-day calendar.

"Persistent?" His voice carries a smile.

"A little bit."

"I can't do anything about that," Cole says. "Other than telling her I'm not available, which I've done several times. I think she's more interested in annoying you than she is in pursuing me. If you don't react to her, she'll give up."

I consider his words and nod. "You may be right. I'll work on it."

Cole lifts my chin with his finger, looking into my eyes. "Can you work on one more thing? Be more careful and not take so many risks? Don't get me wrong; I like your courage and sense of justice. But putting yourself in danger is not the answer."

Before I can respond, Cole tips my face up for a kiss, and the warmth of the sun is like a blessing.

Cole sits back and sighs. "We need to go," and regret is in his voice.

He stands and grabs my hand, pulling me to my feet. "C'mon," he says, and I'm relieved by his genuine grin. "I'll race you to the truck."

As we drive back to Justice, I realize not only did God protect me from Outlaw, but He also protected my relationship with Cole.

He catches me watching him. "What?"

I reach over to slide my hand down his arm. "Nothing. Just happy."

Cole gives me the sweet, slow smile that always makes my stomach flip a little.

"Me too."

12

"Ah-oooooo." I bolt upright, and for a terrifying second, imagine Outlaw must be right outside my window. The sound reverberates again, and I realize this is not Outlaw's scream. Instead, the distinctive baying of hound dogs fills the air. There must be dozens. I glance at Tweety and realize it's only 5 a.m.

Ugh. Once again, I regret my impulsiveness. Last night Sly arranged a ride with True North for the 'Colossal Cougar Caper' as Maggie called it. I'd volunteered to go with them. What was I thinking?

Sly is hoping to interview True and detail his process of tracking Outlaw. The *Voice of Justice* promised to put her story on the front page.

"Above the fold," Sly said last night after talking to the editor. Her awed tone made it sound like they had nominated her for an Emmy or something. I nodded like I knew what she was talking about and decided to Google it later.

"*Sly*," I remind myself. "*I'm doing it for Sly.*"

I meet Maggie in the hall and smile at her sleepy grouchiness.

"What's going on?" she grumbles.

Before I can answer, Sly emerges from the bathroom.

"Maggie, what are you doing up?" Sly is dressed in jeans, a green thermal, and a denim shirt tied around her hips. Her short, dark hair is spiked in all the right places.

"Dogs." Maggie gripes. "Loud."

A smile twitches around Sly's mouth. "Well, try to go back to sleep. Rachel's mom won't be here until 9:00 a.m. to pick you up."

Jealousy swamps me as Maggie does an about-face and returns to her bed. Since it's Columbus Day, there's no school for either of us. I had planned to sleep until noon.

I follow Sly downstairs to the kitchen. My fleeting hope of warm and waiting pancakes evaporates when I notice she's only started the coffee.

Caffeine. When Sly fills an enormous container with coffee, then holds the carafe up to me, I grab for it. I'm going to need lots today, so I might as well get started.

"We're not leaving the truck, right?" I ask.

"No," Sly adds cream to the coffee and fastens the lid on the bottle. "Don't worry. Nick already gave me the lecture. 'Stay in the truck.' Sly lowers her voice to imitate Nick's tone. 'If True goes off on a trail, call me, and I'll come and pick you up. I don't want you two out there alone with lions, and hunters, and dogs.'"

"Oh my." I laugh, thinking of the line from the Wizard of Oz.

"Those were my very words," Sly grins. "Nick was not amused."

She eyes my pajamas decorated in happy penguins engaged in various winter sports activities. "I see you're dressed for success." She smiles as she packs a bag with sandwiches and fruit for our lunch.

I set down the coffee pot and ask, "Could you pour me a cup to go while I get dressed? Ten minutes, I promise."

"Sure," Sly agrees. "But remember True said he's leaving at 6:00 a.m. sharp, with or without us.

"With us," I promise, my words floating down the stairway.

6:00 a.m.

THE BARKING of the dogs is deafening as we pull into the grade school parking lot. Trucks of every size, color, and vintage fill the space, but Sly spots True North's Range Rover and parks nearby. Nick and True stand alongside the truck while a black-and-tan hound paces between them.

Nick introduces us to True, who simply grunts in reply. An awkward silence follows, then Sly, ever the diplomat asks, "What's your dog's name?"

True chews on a toothpick hanging from the corner of his mouth. He stares at Sly, probably deciding if she's worth the effort of an answer.

Finally, he says, "Rover."

"Original," I mutter and immediately regret it when True pierces me with his dark eyes.

He turns to Nick. "The sass is strong with this one."

"You have no idea," Nick agrees, and I glare at him.

Rover saves me from responding when he tips back his head and emits a loud and mournful cry. The other trackers' dogs respond, and I barely catch True's words when he spits out his toothpick, slaps both palms on his thighs, and announces, "Time to hunt."

Minutes later, we're hurtling up the mountain in a weird, howling dog parade.

"Worthless," True mutters as he passes several trucks. "They'll only be in my way." It seems True is not a team player.

Sly and I sit in the row of seats behind True while Rover

rides in the cargo area. Sly hands me her phone to use for voice recording. Then she pulls out a notebook and pen.

"So, Mr. North, can you tell me a little about your history with the cougar you call Outlaw?"

I hold the phone closer and hope this is a brief interview. My arm will get tired pretty fast.

"Call me True. Mr. North was my Pappy." True touches the electric window control, and when it lowers, he turns and spits out the window. The wind whistles, and I watch, horrified as the glob hangs in midair then floats backward. Directly toward me.

The window control whirs, raising it precisely in time to catch the slimy stuff. It hits the window and slides down the glass.

"Humph," True gripes. "Guess my aim's off today."

I try not to wonder what that means. Then I'm relieved when Sly scoots across the seat and tugs me away from True's window. Who knows how many more times he'll practice his aim on this trip?

"Well, let's see," True starts his story, and I'm glad for the distraction. "I met that son-of-a ... gun ... about this time last year. He'd been hasslin' some tourists up near Yellowstone, and nobody could catch him. That's when they called me."

True glances over his shoulder at the phone I'm holding. "This comin' through loud and clear, missy?" he asks.

"Yes, sir," I say.

He eyes me suspiciously but turns back to the road. "Alrighty."

He glances in the rearview mirror, and I swivel to see that now we're the only truck on the road. The other trackers have taken side roads deeper into the forest.

"I tracked that cat for three days, me and my dog, Pepper." The crack in his voice when he mentions his dog makes my throat tighten in sympathy.

"It was gettin' on near dusk when Pepper treed him." True sounds as if he's reliving the experience. "I was about to pull the trigger when the cougar dropped. At first, I thought I'd taken the shot after all. But no, Outlaw had taken his chances with Pepper."

True swings the Range Rover onto a barely visible dirt road and continues. "Course, I couldn't take the shot without possibly hitting Pepper. So, I waded into the fight, using my rifle butt to knock him off my dog. But I was too late. The cougar had torn Pepper's throat open, and I knew there was no way she'd survive."

Beside me, Sly gives a slight sniffle, and I fight back tears. True is quiet for a minute, then says, "Well, I guess I lost my mind. I grabbed my knife and tore into the cat. Pepper had already injured him. She went down fighting, that's for sure.

I should have shot the cat, but somehow, I didn't want to make it that easy for him. I wanted him to hurt. I stabbed him, but he was quick. He turned and took a vicious swipe at me and almost cost me my eye. So, I took his."

He speaks those last words with such satisfaction and hatred I shiver and move closer to Sly.

"Why did Outlaw come into Justice? Isn't it rare for a cougar to go near people?" Sly waits with her pen poised for his answer, even as I hold the phone closer. I want to know the answer too.

"Hah, that one, he makes his own rules. That's why I call him Outlaw. Or could be he met me face-to-face and got a taste for humans."

I shiver at these words and the ones that follow.

"But he'll learn better soon enough."

"We're here." True parks the vehicle, clambers out, and releases Rover from the cargo area. The dog is barking and panting, obviously eager to be on the trail.

Sly opens her door, but I grab her arm. "You promised you'd stay in the truck," I remind her. For once, I'm the cautious one.

She frowns and pulls the door closed with a slam. True reappears to open the driver's door and lean in.

"You two girlies stay here. I promised Deputy Nick I'd keep you safe, and he doesn't 'peer to be a man I wanna cross. If you need to take care of business, trees are over there." He nods to a thicket of trees about 50 yards away. "Make it quick, and you'll be fine."

Then True North and Rover disappear into the woods, leaving us alone with no clue where we are.

"Well, this is a fine mess you've gotten us into, Ollie." I try to make Sly laugh by quoting Daddy's favorite line from an old black-and-white movie.

She ignores me as she transcribes the notes from True's interview. When True pulled onto this back road, we lost cell service, but I have the Candy Crush app, and I'm prepared to crush some candy. The app opens, drawing me into the colorful, musical world.

"That's really annoying." Sly doesn't glance up from her notebook.

I dig in my bag for earbuds, but her following words stop me.

"Anyway, we should conserve your battery in case we need to call for help."

I resist the urge to ask why she isn't worried about conserving her battery. I understand she wants to listen to the recording and take notes while it's fresh in her mind. Slumping into the seat, I close my eyes and try to nap.

"I have to go to the bathroom." The need has gone from eventual to urgent.

Sly nibbles her lower lip and peers around. After True left, she moved the vehicle closer to the trees in case this became an issue. But fallen branches lay all around, and she couldn't drive closer without chancing a flat tire. So, we're still at least 15 yards from the closet cover.

"C'mon, I'll go with you," Sly offers.

"No, one of us should wait in the car and stay alive," I protest.

Sly rolls her eyes but nods. As I race toward the trees, she calls, "Remember, leaves of three, let them be."

Five minutes later, I'm back, and as Sly pours water over my hands, I observe, "Well, that was unpleasant."

"I bet," she says with a distinct lack of sympathy. "I'm glad I have the bladder of a camel."

She holds out the container. "Coffee?"

I shrug and take the bottle. "Why not?"

I'm about to pour coffee into a Styrofoam cup when the first rifle shot echoes around us.

Coffee splashes over my jeans, but since we bought a cheap bottle the liquid is only lukewarm.

I replace the container lid just as another shot reverberates.

Sly and I speak in unison. "Outlaw."

We listen for more shots, shouts, or even Rover barking, but there's nothing. Five minutes pass into ten, then fifteen. After thirty excruciating minutes, a faint bark draws our attention. True and Rover are loping toward us.

True loads his dog and rifle into the cargo area and climbs into the driver's seat. Without a word, he swings the Range Rover around, and soon we're on the highway, back to Justice.

I open my mouth, but Sly beats me to it.

"True, did you find Outlaw?" She asks.

He doesn't respond, so I try. "True, what happened? Where's the cougar?"

True grinds his teeth, and for a minute, I assume he's not going to answer.

"Outlaw is dead. Tracked him to a cliff, shot him, and he fell into the river. That's all I'm gonna say, so don't go jawin' at me for more."

He rolls down the window, and I duck and slide as far away as possible. This time the glob sails out on the wind. Then he raises the glass, and for the next thirty minutes, the only sound in the car is Sly's pen scribbling furiously on her notepad.

When we drive into cell range, Sly discreetly texts Nick to tell him what happened. Afterward, she silences her phone in case Nick tries to call her. If we break the silence, True will probably stop and dump us out, leaving us to walk home.

True clenches and unclenches his jaw, and I'm puzzled by his expression. For a year, he's chased Outlaw, the same animal that almost took True's eye and killed his beloved dog. But he's showing no relief or satisfaction. He's furious. Why?

My own emotions are confused too. I love animals and find cougars to be beautiful and graceful. But Outlaw crossed the line when he started threatening people and pets. I shudder, thinking of Joey's innocent face. Although I'm sad True killed the cougar, I know he had no other choice.

We pull into the school parking lot to hear cars honking and people cheering. True parks the truck, and as we climb out, the mayor himself arrives to shake True's hand.

"Ms. Thomas, let's take a picture to go with your story in the *Voice of Justice*." The mayor takes a firm grasp of True's hand, holding on until Sly can record the event.

Sly takes several quick pictures since True's face is getting red with annoyance. Sheriff Herman and Nick join us, and they receive the same abbreviated answer we did when they question True.

"I shot him off the cliff. He died and fell into the river. That's all I got to say."

As True is swept away by the tide of people, one question nags at me.

What really happened on that cliff today?

13

Monday, October 15
6:00 p.m.

Outlaw is the chief topic of conversation over dinner. We decide on an impromptu potluck, which includes Captain Cluck's chicken supplied by Sly and me and two gallons of spaghetti and garlic bread courtesy of Cole and Nick. Grace and Kellen pick up a fruit and veggie tray at the grocery store, and we have a feast.

Maggie is still with Rachel, so it's us three couples, which is nice.

"Now that True killed Outlaw, life can go back to normal," Kellen says as he wraps spaghetti around his fork.

"What is normal like in Justice, Montana?" Grace asks.

"Dunno," Kellen says. "But it sure doesn't include a rogue mountain lion."

"I support that statement," Nick says with a glance at Sly. I don't think he's recovered from the knowledge we were so close to Outlaw today. I know I haven't.

"I guess it's kind of fitting True was the one who tracked Outlaw," Cole says.

"Yes," agrees Nick. "But I wish he'd recovered the body. It would help to know if Outlaw had rabies."

"If Outlaw is dead, then why is that important?" I ask, determinedly pulling the battered skin from my chicken thigh and placing it on the edge of my plastic plate. Then, I see Cole reach to move the crunchy goodness to his plate.

"Outlaw had several encounters with wild animals. He tried to go after a few pets and horses but never drew blood. But if he had rabies, we may need to be on the lookout for other animals he bit."

Nick piles his plate with a second helping of spaghetti and glances at Sly. "How did the interview go with True? He told me about his history with Outlaw, but I wasn't sure he'd open up for the newspaper. Did he give you any background?"

"Yes," Sly says. "True told us all about it today."

Since Cole, Grace, and Kellen haven't heard it, she repeats the story of how True and Pepper tracked Outlaw.

"True couldn't take a shot for fear of hitting Pepper, so he charged the cougar with a knife. He slashed the cat in his eye right as Outlaw scratched True and gave him that nasty scar."

"An eye for an eye," Grace says.

"Exactly. After that, Outlaw ran off, leaving True to carry Pepper to the truck which was several miles away." Sly says.

"Wait, don't trackers use more than one dog?" Kellen asks.

"Most do," Nick agrees. "But True told me he and Pepper were a team, and they didn't need any help. Unfortunately, Pepper died in True's arms, and True almost lost his eye. He's been chasing Outlaw all around Montana ever since. Maybe after this, True can get some closure and move on."

After we clean the kitchen, we move to the living room to watch Monday night football. The Denver Broncos are playing the Atlanta Falcons, and this game is personal. The McBride and Thomas families support the Broncos, but since Grace is from Atlanta, her team is the Falcons. Kellen agrees to side with her in a real show of boyfriend loyalty.

At half time Nick leaves for his shift at the sheriff's department. As Sly follows him outside to say goodbye, Grace gives me a soft smile. "They are perfect together," she says.

Cole and Kellen are in the kitchen refilling the popcorn bowl, so I'm free enough to say, "I know, right? I'm so happy for her. I've always felt guilty she left college to take care of Maggie and me instead of starting her own life. She deserves this." I consider telling Grace about my conversation with Maggie but decide to keep it between us.

The guys return, and soon we're caught up in the game. Afterward, Cole and I accept our loss, promising the Broncs will make a comeback.

When everyone leaves, Sly sits beside me on the couch, her frown alerting me to bad news.

"What's wrong?" I ask.

"Nothing. But Nick wanted us to know Sheriff Herman reopened the investigation into Mamma and Daddy's accident."

"If it was an accident," I correct.

"Yes," she says. "Nick wants us prepared for whatever they find, even if it's nothing."

"How can it be nothing?" I demand. "I mean, there's the letter Daddy wrote days before they were murdered," I state bitterly.

Sly winces at the word *murdered* and cautions me. "Please be careful what you say, Jess. We can't go around accusing Anthony Avery without evidence."

"Nick will find it," I say with confidence.

"He's doing everything he can. And Nick says the FBI has their eyes on Anthony Avery for crimes connected to his building inspections."

"That's not enough," I snap. "Avery needs to be punished for what he did to Mamma and Daddy. What he did to all of us!" My voice breaks, and Sly leans to hug me.

"I agree. But we have to take justice where we find it. If the

FBI can build a case against him, Anthony Avery will go to prison."

"But not for killing our parents," I say.

Sly shakes her head, and I see the sadness in her eyes. She's been so strong for Maggie and me, and now I realize she always comforts me, while I rarely comfort her.

"I understand," I say, acknowledging deep inside I don't. "I'll accept whatever happens." Then, giving her a quick hug, I turn to go to my room, telling her I need to finish some homework.

For nearly an hour, I sit on my bed, contemplating the difference between justice and revenge. My American Lit book is open but forgotten as I take the time to examine my heart and admit the truth.

I want revenge.

14

"Jess, could you do me a favor?" Sly is standing at the front door when Grace drops me off from school. Her short hair sticks out in several directions as if she's been running her fingers through it. A lot.

"I promised Mrs. Irving she could borrow our ice cream freezer this evening for her granddaughter's birthday party, and I realized she'll be leaving the office soon. Would you be willing to run it over to her?" Sly holds out the box, anticipating my yes.

Mrs. Irving is the receptionist at the Beaverhead County Building Inspector's office where Daddy worked. After our parents' deaths, she was so kind, bringing food several times a week for over a month. She even helped Sly set up a system to manage our finances. At 22, that had been an overwhelming challenge for Sly, and she continues a close bond with Mrs. Irving.

"Sure." I take the box from her. "Are you okay?"

"Yes, I'm a little stressed trying to finish this article for the print edition of the newspaper. The editor needs it by 5:00 p.m., and I'm running behind. This will help a lot. Thanks."

Sly hurries off to the kitchen, where she's set up her computer.

I follow her to grab an apple from the bowl on the kitchen table. Then I lift the car keys from the hook near the back door.

"Road trip," I sing as I hurry to Sly's Honda. I've only had my license a few weeks, so I appreciate any opportunity I get to drive alone.

I consider calling Grace to make the twenty-minute trip with me, but I remember she's babysitting the twins this afternoon while Mrs. Ellison has a hair appointment.

The office is in Dillon, and I enjoy the drive, taking time to appreciate the beautiful fall colors. Soon, snow will cover Montana, but now I soak up the lingering display of autumn.

Mrs. Irving is all smiles when I deliver the ice cream freezer.

"Jess, what a treat." Mrs. Irving hurries around her desk to envelop me in a warm hug.

"It's nice to see you too," I reply. "How is Mr. Irving feeling? Sly told me he had a mild heart attack last month."

"He's much better. He's enjoying his retirement and spending more time with the grandkids. Thank you for sharing the freezer. Tonight is Audra's fifth birthday, and she'll be so excited to have homemade ice cream."

Mrs. Irving places the freezer on the floor and takes my hands in hers. "How are you girls doing?" The question is simple, but her compassionate gaze causes my throat to tighten.

"We're good." My answer is as simple, but I can see she understands the deeper meaning. "We're healing."

"I'm relieved to learn the cougar is no longer a threat. I worried about you girls."

"It was exciting for a few days," I agree. "Sly is writing up her account of everything that happened. It should be in the newspaper tomorrow."

"I'll look forward to reading it," Mrs. Irving assures me.

I turn to go, and Mrs. Irving touches my arm, "Jess, your parents would be so proud of you girls, all three of you."

A glimmer of tears shines in her eyes, and I manage a brief nod but can only respond, "Thank you."

As I leave, I push open the wooden door and walk into a man trying to enter.

"Hey, watch it," the man says, and I glance up, startled to see Anthony Avery standing there.

Before I can respond, his already scowling expression turns darker as he says, "Jess Thomas," in a way that makes me take a step back. "What are you doing here?"

So many emotions flood through me—anger, fear, sorrow. I'd just been thinking of the times I'd visited this office with my dad. Now I'm face to face with the man I suspect may have killed my parents.

Anthony Avery takes advantage of my momentary confusion and moves closer. "You know, Ms. Thomas, let me give you some valuable advice. You should always be careful where you're going. If you don't, you might get hurt. Accidents happen every day."

I stare, and he nods at the door and says with a sneer. "You never know what kind of trouble might be waiting on the other side."

Did Anthony Avery threaten me? Anger wells deep inside, and before I can stop myself, I say, "I know what you did, and I have the proof. And even more, God knows what you did. So, I'm asking God for justice for my family, Mr. Avery. I believe He will give it."

Something flickers in his eyes. Fear?

Excellent.

As I walk away, my trembling legs threaten to buckle. But I square my shoulders, signaling to Anthony Avery that he doesn't scare me.

Now, if I can only convince myself.

As I turn onto our road, I pass Nick in his squad car. I give a friendly wave, and he nods but doesn't smile. Weird.

Maggie is sitting on the porch when I arrive home, and she pulls me down beside her.

"Don't go in there," she warns, biting her lip.

"I know. Sly is finishing up her story on True and Outlaw. I'll stay out of her way."

"No, that's not it," Maggie confides. "She sent that in about thirty minutes ago, just before Nick showed up."

"Yeah, I passed Nick on the way home. Did something happen? Does he have news about the investigation into Daddy and Mamma's accident?" I stand, but Maggie grabs my hand.

"No, he said he didn't know anything yet. But I could tell he wanted to talk privately, so I came out here to do my homework. A few minutes later, Nick slammed through the door and drove off. I asked Sly what happened and ..." Maggie's voice trails off.

"What?"

"She was crying." Maggie brushes her tears away and turns to me. "Sly hardly ever cries. Even when Mamma and Daddy died, she cried the first night, then said she would be strong for you and me. Remember?"

I nod, wondering if that was such a wise plan after all. Sly left college to care for Maggie and me and overnight became the head of the house. That's a lot of responsibility for a young woman.

"Did you ask Sly what's wrong?"

Maggie shakes her head, her russet brown hair swirling around her freckled face.

"I didn't want to bother her. But I think it must be something with Nick, don't you?"

I nibble my lower lip, reflecting Maggie's unease.

"I guess so. When I passed Nick, he barely responded when I waved. Now that I think about it, his mouth was tight like it gets when he's mad."

"Why would he be mad at Sly? She's perfect."

I smile at her defense of our big sister. "Don't worry, Magpie. It's probably nothing, just their first argument. Every couple has them, even Cole and me."

Maggie grins. "Don't you mean, 'especially Cole and you'?"

"We're getting better," I assure her. "We haven't argued in over a week."

Maggie starts to say something, probably about my adventure with Daisy and Outlaw, but I interrupt. "Let's start some grilled cheese sandwiches and tomato soup for dinner. That's one of Sly's favorites."

Maggie hops to her feet and follows me into the house where we put together the meal.

But, when I knock on Sly's bedroom door, announcing dinner, she responds with a muffled, "You girls eat. I'm not hungry."

I return to the kitchen and shake my head at Maggie's questioning gaze.

As we eat in silence, I consider my earlier plan to tell Sly about today's meeting with Anthony Avery. I shiver a little as I remember his words. *"You should always be careful where you are going. If you don't, you might get hurt. Accidents happen every day."* Those are almost the exact words he said to Daddy.

But I can't tell Sly when she's so upset with Nick. And I don't want to tell Nick, although I'm sure I should. Somehow that feels disloyal to my sister.

As I dip the edge of my sandwich into my soup, I consider my options. It's not like Anthony Avery will try to hurt me, right? He doesn't know we asked Nick to investigate the accident.

By the time I finish my dinner, I'm convinced I'm overreacting to Avery's words.

He's just trying to intimidate me. I have nothing to worry about.

15

"Your brother made my sister cry." I try to keep accusation out of my voice but judging by Cole's startled expression, I fail.

"He did?"

I roll my eyes and barely stop from muttering, 'clueless.'

"Yes, he did." I cross my arms and gaze out the window of the truck, pretending a deep fascination with the countryside.

Cole swings the truck onto the road that leads to Pastor Jarrod and Anna's house. I had mixed feelings when Cole asked if he could drive me tonight. I want to spend time with him, of course, but I'm also mad at his brother for hurting my sister.

"Why?" Cole asks.

"I don't know, you tell me. I asked Sly, but she won't say." Frustration colors my tone.

Cole glances over, raising one eyebrow. "But you think my brother took me out for a latte to talk about his relationship problems?"

"Don't be sexist," I snap, but I glance away, so Cole misses my reluctant grin. For a second, I picture Nick and Cole sitting in a cozy booth at Rosie's Beans and Greens, eating salads and drinking frothy coffees. An unexpected snort escapes, and I cover it with a cough.

"Hey." Cole reaches over to touch my arm, and I turn to him. "I'm sorry Nick said something to hurt Sly, but I don't know anything about it. I saw Nick having a deep discussion with my dad the other night, and it seemed pretty serious, but I didn't ask questions."

"Really?" I say, tucking that piece of information away for further examination.

"It may have nothing to do with Sly, though. Let's give them space to figure it out on their own without letting it affect us. Agreed?"

"I guess you're right," I agree. "But if you find out anything, you'll let me know, right?"

Cole pulls the truck into Pastor Jarrod's lane. "I will," he agrees. "As long as Nick doesn't force me to pinky swear not to tell you."

"Hilarious," I mutter as I release my seat belt, but I fight a giggle at the thought of Nick and Cole, pinky's locked, making promises.

When Cole parks the truck in Pastor Jarrod's driveway, I'm surprised to see a bonfire flickering in the side yard.

"Were we supposed to bring food?" Cole asks.

"Not that I remember," I say.

We make our way past Anna's rose bushes and over to join the group, who are sitting on blankets and logs near the fire.

"Surprise," Anna calls as she spots us. "Jarrod and I decided at the last minute to move the group out here tonight. Now that the cougar is no longer a threat, we want to enjoy one of the last few pleasant nights of fall."

She hands each of us a cup of apple cider and motions for us to find a seat. Cole nods to where Grace and Kellen are sitting

on a log, and we join them. Grace and I sit in the middle with
the guys on either side of us.

As everyone settles, I notice a Jeep driving up the lane to the
house. All the BOB members are here, so I'm curious about this
unexpected visitor.

A tiny gasp escapes when I realize who has arrived.

Mark Crowley.

I haven't seen Mark in several weeks, not since Cole and I
confronted him in the hospital. Although he apologized for
kidnapping me and the subsequent car accident, it's still strange
to see him here.

Pastor Jarrod walks across the yard to greet him, and Grace
turns to me with a silent question. I answer with a shrug. We both
watch in fascination as Pastor Jarrod and Mark approach the fire.

Mark told us he was meeting with Pastor Jarrod when he was
in the hospital, and now it's obvious they're developing a solid
friendship.

"Hey, guys," Pastor Jarrod addresses the group. "Let's
welcome Mark Crowley to Bunch of Believers."

I peek up at Mark, and his grin says it all.

Cole is the first to stand, and he crosses to shake hands with
Mark.

"Welcome to the family."

Across from us, Caleb settles onto a blanket, strums his
guitar, and soon we are singing.

Caleb begins with the simple melody, "Hallelujah." When we
reach the line, "Lord, I love you," Mark's voice joins with ours. I
try to focus on singing, but I can't take my eyes off Mark. He's
lost the anger that used to define him. He's sitting cross-legged
on the ground, eyes closed, and his relaxed face radiates peace.

After several more songs, Pastor Jarrod stands and nods
at me.

"Jess, I apologize for not asking ahead of time, so if you aren't
comfortable sharing, I understand. But I heard about how God

protected you and Joey from Outlaw. Are you willing to tell us what happened?"

I flush, thinking about my unauthorized ride on Daisy. But I'm more than happy to discuss the miracle.

"It terrified me," I say. "All I could think of was how scared Joey must be. Janey said the searchers were looking in the wrong place, so I reacted and saddled Daisy.

When we saw Outlaw, Daisy started bucking, and I almost fell. Poor Daisy nearly bolted, and I can't blame her. But if I had fallen, there would be no way to escape the cougar."

"But God."

Grace's soft words make me smile as she repeats my mamma's favorite saying.

"Yes. But God. Just as Outlaw was ready to attack, something glittered in the leaves, and I realized Joey was hiding there. When Outlaw leaped for Joey, I screamed, "Help us, God."

One minute Outlaw was in the air, and the next, he was staggering around like he'd hit a brick wall. Then, finally, he turned and ran away."

Of course, I don't mention that Outlaw looked back at me with a promise of next time. I'm thankful I don't have to worry anymore.

"That's amazing," Anna says. "God protected you both."

I nod and glance around at my friends, the people I love, contentment surging through me. Cole reaches for my hand and laces his fingers through mine.

"There's one more piece of business to discuss before we make s'mores," Pastor Jarrod says.

"Jacquie Edwards called today and asked if we would help chaperone the junior high group's trip to Bannack this Saturday. I understand this is late notice, but the park will close for the season after this weekend, so this is the only chance. The weather will be nice too."

"That sounds like fun," Terri says. "I love that old town. There's so much history."

"Do you need any drivers?" Caleb offers.

"Yes," Pastor Jarrod says. "We'll meet at the church at 11:15, so we can assign drivers and riders when we see how many are coming."

"Jess and I work until noon, but we can go from there." Cole glances over at me, and I nod.

"Perfect. We're leaving Justice at 11:30 a.m., so we'll only be a little ahead of you. The junior high parents are providing lunch and drinks for us, and we plan to eat when we first arrive, then explore for a few hours."

We fill the rest of the evening with excited planning, anticipating one more outing before winter. I'm relieved we can move around again without the threat of being attacked by Outlaw. So far, the trackers can't find his body, and we accept that may never happen. But at least he's no longer a threat to the people I love. I'm satisfied with that outcome.

16

Friday, October 19
6:00 p.m.

"Do you have plans tonight?" I casually ask Sly as we wash the dinner dishes. She made her famous meatloaf tonight. She also baked two pies, muffins, and had cinnamon rolls rising on the counter. Sly bakes when she's upset. I figure if she and Nick don't make up soon, I'll need a special shopping trip to Missoula for larger clothes.

"No."

I try again. "Tomorrow?"

She sighs and dries her hands on a towel. "Let's talk."

I'm startled by her invitation but nod and join her at the kitchen table. Maggie is at a sleepover, and Cole and I are going to the football game with Grace and Kellen later. It hurts to think of leaving Sly here all alone. In pain.

"Nick wants to join the FBI."

For a minute, I'm speechless, but that seldom lasts long.

"What?" I squeak.

Now that Sly is ready to share, the words rush out.

"When Nick worked with the FBI last month on the

arrest of Robert Sinclair, he caught the leading special agent's attention. He said Nick would be a great fit for the FBI, and he volunteered to guide him through the long process. There's a lot involved, so that's a very generous offer."

"But I thought Nick was planning to run for Sheriff when Herman retires next year."

Sly shrugs. "That was the plan. But since talking to Special Agent Morris, Nick is interested in this opportunity. He came over the other night to discuss it with me, but I'm afraid I reacted badly."

"I doubt that," I say. "I'm sure it was a shock."

Sly gives a rueful laugh. "Oh, it was." She sighs and makes a tiny crease in the tablecloth. "Nick and I have only been dating for a month, so of course, he doesn't owe me any explanation of his future plans."

I protest, but she shakes her head to silence me.

"That's exactly what I said to him," she confesses.

"Ouch."

"Yeah. That was Nick's reaction." Sly sighs and makes another crease in the cloth. "He looked like I slapped him. The excitement left his face, and he said, 'I just thought you should know.' Then he walked away."

I'm not sure if Sly is aware she is crying. Instead, she stares at Grandma Thomas's floral tablecloth as if she might find some words of wisdom written there.

"I'm sorry." I reach over to touch her hand. "Have you talked to him since then?"

Sly shakes her head, swiping at her eyes. "No, and I don't expect to. I was almost cruel to him. But I felt like I had to protect my heart. We've already lost so much. Maybe this needed to happen now before we all got too attached." Sly's voice cracks, and I hurry around the table to gather my sister into my arms as she cries.

An hour later, I climb into Cole's truck. I'm wearing a little makeup to cover the evidence of my conversation with Sly, but it doesn't fool Cole.

"You talked to Sly?"

"Yes. Did you talk to Nick?"

Cole nods and pulls out of the driveway, heading to the football stadium. The plan is to meet Grace and Kellen for the game and go out for pizza afterward.

But plans can change, I think cynically, and I must make a sound because Cole pulls into the parking lot of the Methodist Church and turns off the engine.

"Jess, we're not going to let this come between us," Cole says with conviction.

"We're not?" I give a tentative smile. "Are you positive?"

"I'm positive I'll do everything I can to make that true." Cole's gaze is serious. "Will you?"

"I want to, but I hate to see her hurting."

"I get that. Nick is hurting too."

I wrinkle my nose. "Really? He just dumped my sister for the FBI."

"No, he didn't." Cole's tone is adamant. "He wanted to discuss a possibility for their future, but Sly made it plain she wasn't interested."

At my outraged look, he adds, "Hey, I get it. Sly is 23 years old, and Nick is 29. She's still growing into her responsibilities of being guardian to you and Maggie. That's a lot. It makes sense she isn't ready for a committed relationship."

"You're joking, right?" I snap. "Sly may be young, but she is a mature, grown woman—she has to be. And here's a news flash, Cole. Sly is in love with Nick. In. Love. Not a crush, not a casual fling. She's never been like this with other boyfriends or even her former fiancé."

Cole's confusion is apparent. "Then why did she tell Nick to have a nice life without her?"

"I don't know all of it," I admit. "But Nick did kind of pull the rug out from under her. She thought he was planning to stay in the area and become the sheriff in a few years. Overnight Nick changed everything, and she reacted to protect her heart. And maybe to protect Maggie and me from getting hurt."

I see the moment Cole gets it.

"Nick can be dense sometimes," he mutters.

"You think?" I turn to stare out the window, but I'm surprised when Cole reaches over to unlock my seat belt.

"Come here," he invites me. "Please."

The tension eases from my body as I slide across to lean against Cole's chest, his arms wrapping around me. I smell the pine aftershave he wears, and I want to forget about our siblings' problems and just be us. Together.

We sit like that for a minute, not speaking. Then, finally, Cole leans down to kiss the top of my head.

"As much as we might want to, we can't fix their lives. That's up to them and God. But let's make an agreement."

I look up. "What kind of agreement?"

"We naturally defend our siblings. That's a given. But I don't want it to cause trouble between us, too. So, let's stay out of it. Deal?"

I consider his statement about staying out of it, then scrap my plan to set Nick and Sly up to 'accidentally' be in the same place.

"Deal," I agree.

"C'mon." He gives me one last hug. "Grace and Kellen will think we ditched them."

When we arrive at the football stadium, the parking lot is already packed. Football is a big deal in Justice, plus this is senior recognition night, so the crowd is larger than usual.

We find Grace and Kellen in the rowdy group, saving us seats on the first row of bleachers.

"Whew," Grace says when I scrunch in next to her. "I was worried we'd have to sit on each other's laps if you didn't get here soon."

"Thank you for getting the seats." Cole settles on my other side and nods to Kellen.

From the seat behind me, Terri taps my shoulder. "Look at Macy," she urges. "Doesn't she look adorable?"

I scan the area at one end of the stadium, where a portable wooden platform sits. Caleb is talking to Mr. Simmons, the athletic director, while Macy searches the crowd for us. When she spots us, she waves discreetly but Terri, Grace, and I stand and yell, "Macy!"

I can see her blush from here, and I grin. If she's going to become a famous singer, she'll eventually get used to having fans yell her name. Macy is wearing boyfriend jeans rolled at the ankle, tan booties, a white T, and a cropped cardigan in a gorgeous cranberry color. Her blonde hair waves around her shoulders, and she looks terrific.

"Ladies and gentlemen, please stand as Caleb Williams and Macy Scott lead us in the national anthem."

Caleb waits for the crowd to quiet then begins to strum his guitar. He's positioned a microphone to amplify the instrument, and another sits between Caleb and Macy.

The moment they begin to sing, chills run down my arms as their voices blend beautifully. Beside me, Cole has removed his hat, and we join the others in placing our hands over our hearts.

When the song ends, the crowd erupts in cheers, and I'm thrilled for Caleb and Macy as they leave the stage. They have something special, and I hope they will continue to sing together.

As I settle in to enjoy the game, I think about the trip we'll take to Bannack tomorrow. Although we'll be working in the morning, I'll be able to spend the entire afternoon with Cole. It's going to be amazing.

17

Saturday, October 20
12:00 p.m.

When I finish work for the morning, I use the women's restroom to change into clean clothes. I pull on my favorite plaid shirt with the deep green stripe that matches my eyes. Then, smoothing my wayward curls back into my braid, I add a touch of lip gloss and call it done.

Cole gives me a slow smile when I climb into the cab.

"Nice shirt."

I turn to buckle my seat belt and try to hide my blush.

As we leave the foothills behind, I'm glad Cole's driving. The mountain road is narrow with sharp twists and curves, and I hook my arm over Roxie's middle so she doesn't slide into Cole.

The picnic is in full swing when we arrive in Bannack. I shiver a little as I remember the last time I was here when Mark kidnapped me. I wonder if Cole is thinking about that event too. But he seems focused on the sandwiches, chips, and cookies laid out on a picnic table. Fortunately, he's distracted by the food. We've had a relaxed morning, and I don't want any awkwardness to spoil it now.

Maggie waves when she sees us and gestures to the blanket where she and Rachel are sitting, surrounded by the remains of their lunch.

"Here." Maggie points to a stack of sandwiches and two bags of chips. "I snagged these before they were all gone."

"Thanks, Magpie," Cole says, ruffling her hair. "I'm starved." He proves that by devouring his first sandwich in about two-and-a-half bites. It disappears before I even unwrap my sandwich.

"So, what's the plan?" Cole pinches off a generous piece of his second sandwich and feeds it to Roxie, who lounges nearby. Then he opens his bag of chips and slides a few into his sandwich. Cole is an efficient eater.

"Rachel and I are going to the schoolhouse and take turns being the teacher."

Teaching is Maggie's dream, and she always enjoys visiting the old schoolhouse. The last time our family was in Bannack, Maggie persuaded us to be her students. Mamma, Sly, and I had fit in the cramped, wooden desks, but Daddy had to sit on a bench alongside Mamma.

When Maggie caught him whispering something to Mamma during her 'lesson,' she had primly asked if he wanted to sit in the dunce chair that waited in the corner of the room.

"My apologies, Miss Thomas," Daddy had said. "I promise not to interrupt again."

I smile now at the memory.

"Are you going to eat those?" Cole motions to my unopened chips, and I hand them over.

"Apparently not," I say with a grin.

A few minutes later, we clean up the lunch trash, and Jacquie gives instructions for the afternoon. "You're free to explore on your own, or you can join one of the guided tours that start every half hour. Restrooms are in the gift shop, although there are outhouses at either end of the town. Meet in the parking lot at 4:00 p.m. for the drive back to Justice. Please respect the property. They have preserved these buildings for many years. Let's leave them the way we found them."

The junior high kids scatter in every direction, and Jacquie turns to the chaperones.

"We'll divide the town into sections. Cole and Jess, you can take the east end of town, and Grace and Kellen, you take the west. Terri and Macy, you stay between the church and the post office. Caleb and Todd can monitor the school and cemetery. Pastor Jarrod will walk through the town while Anna and I keep an eye on the shoppers in the gift store."

We leave for our assigned duties, and soon the town of Bannack echoes with the shouts and laughter of the explorers.

I love visiting this old town and head to the Hotel Meade, my favorite building.

It's a good thing this is our first stop because we catch Trevor and Tyler Adams climbing onto the carved railing of the staircase, ready to take a ride.

"Down. Now." Cole's voice booms, and for a second, I'm afraid the startled boys will fall. But they eye Cole warily and swing their legs back over to stand on the stairs.

"I'm sure Pastor Jarrod said not to slide down the banister. Did you hear that announcement, Jess?"

"I did." I agree.

"We just wanted to have fun." Trevor, the oldest at thirteen, should know better.

"There a difference between fun and breaking your neck. This building and that banister have survived for over 100 years. Do you two want to be known as the brothers who broke Bannack?" Cole's words are lighter, but his tone is still stern.

The boys shake their heads in unison.

"Sorry, Cole," Tyler says, and he sounds sincere. At twelve, he is in Maggie's class at school, and she's told stories about his mischief.

"A group of guys is walking to the cemetery. Why don't you

join them?" Cole suggests, hoping to keep the boys away from the fragile buildings.

"Cool." They run down the stairs and race out the open door.

"Isn't the cemetery in Todd and Caleb's area?" I ask.

Cole grins. "Yep."

Near 3:00 p.m., we see Maggie and Rachel buying candy in the gift shop.

"I figured you two would still be at the schoolhouse," I say.

"Ugh," Rachel grunts in frustration. "Every time we try to go in, there's another big group already there." She hands Maggie one of the red Twizzlers she purchased.

"We're going back now," Maggie says. She takes a determined bite of the red licorice, and I'm concerned for anyone who gets in her way.

"Play nice." Cole grins.

"Of course." Maggie's brown eyes are full of innocence.

The afternoon passes, and when we meet Pastor Jarrod, he says, "Let's gather up any stragglers and head over to the parking lot."

"On it," Cole calls, and we send the students in that direction.

Fifteen minutes later, we gather near the cars, and Pastor Jarrod announces, "Everyone rides back with the same driver. No switching, please."

"I call shotgun!" Aaron Ballantine shouts as he races toward an SUV.

"No way," calls Tinley Adams as she hurries after him. "You were shotgun on the way up."

"I get car sick in the back seat," Aaron says, and their friendly bickering recedes as they climb into the vehicle.

The temperature has dropped, so I'm not surprised to see Maggie's hoodie pulled over her head as Jacquie's car drives away. Unfortunately, Maggie is looking away from me, so she misses my wave. I hope she and Rachel had fun today.

Cole and I are the last to leave, and soon we're winding down the mountain toward Justice.

"I'm beat," I say. "Chasing after those kids all afternoon wore me out."

I lean my head back and close my eyes just as my phone rings. I reach in my backpack to pull it out. "This is Jess."

"Hi Jess, this is Jacquie. Amber wanted to let Maggie know she'll wash her hoodie and bring it to church with her tomorrow."

"I'm confused." I frown. "Maggie is with you. I saw her when you pulled out of the parking lot.".

There is silence for a beat before Jacquie says, "No, Amber and Tiffany are the only girls with me. At lunch, Maggie and Rachel told me that the plan was for them to ride home with you and Cole. Amber borrowed Maggie's hoodie." Jacquie's voice quivers a little, which makes my stomach wobble in response.

I press the speaker option on my phone and say, clearly, "Maggie and Rachel are not in the car with you?"

"No." Jacquie takes a deep breath before she says, "They must still be at Bannack."

Cole doesn't even glance at me but slows the truck and swings onto a broad patch of open grass between the trees. Seconds later, the truck turns back up the mountain, accelerating as much as Cole dares.

"Jacquie, we are five minutes from Bannack and already on our way back," I say.

My mind races with thoughts of Maggie and Rachel all alone in the deserted town. The caretakers left when we did. My heart is pounding so loudly I can barely hear Jacquie when she says, "I feel terrible about this."

Cole speaks up. "They're probably having so much fun they don't even know they're alone. We'll have them in a few minutes, don't worry."

"This is my responsibility," Jacquie says. "I should have

confirmed the plans with you and not assumed they would remember to tell you about the change. I'm so sorry."

I hurry to reassure her. "Jacquie, don't worry. It's a mixup that's easily fixed. I see the church steeple now. We'll be there in a minute."

Gravel crunches under the tires as Cole swings the truck into the lot we left moments earlier.

I reassure Jacquie one more time and end the call. Cole parks the truck, and we jump out, racing toward the old schoolhouse at the far end of the town.

Now that the laughing kids are gone, Bannack earns the designation of *ghost town*.

Roxie is barking, enjoying the race, but she stops and growls as we approach the schoolhouse.

Cole reaches out to grasp my arm and slows my steps.

"Wait."

Roxie's growls deepen, and Cole says, "Good girl, Roxie. Now quiet." Roxie continues to pace, but her growls are more of a low rumble.

Cole puts me behind him as he climbs the wooden steps to the schoolhouse. The door is ajar, and he nudges it so we can slip inside.

At first, I don't understand what I'm seeing. Maggie and Rachel are standing on the platform that holds the teacher's big wooden desk. Maggie's neat handwriting covers the blackboard where she has spelled out her name in cursive. Below is an extensive spelling list. Maggie is a word nerd.

On the other end of the blackboard are basic addition and subtraction problems written in what I assume is Rachel's handwriting. I can imagine the girls taking turns being the schoolmarm and student. But the expressions on their faces don't reflect enjoyment in their game.

Rachel's left arm is white where Maggie is gripping it. In her other hand, Rachel holds a long pointer, waving it back and forth like she's directing a choir. But that's not what's happening. Instead, Rachel is shaking, and the pointer is along for the ride.

Maggie is holding an oversized eraser, raised as if she's about to launch it at something.

My eyes follow their gazes, and my heart stops.

In the corner, about ten feet from the girls, stands a cougar. A one-eyed cougar—Outlaw.

18

I'll never be able to say which animal moved first. All I know is one minute Outlaw and Roxie are feet apart, and the next, they're a snarling, tangled ball in the middle of the room.

"Girls!" Cole's voice is harsh as a whip crack. He avoids the battling animals as he rushes to the girls, urging them toward the door. Rachel is shaking so hard she can't walk, and Cole scoops her up in his arms without breaking stride. Maggie trails a little, peeking over her shoulder at the two animals locked in combat.

"Roxie." Maggie's wail echoes in the room, but Cole ignores her, pushing all three of us through the door. Then he slams it shut, closing himself inside.

"Cole!" I pound on the door, but he holds it closed.

"Jess, go to the back and open that door, then you and the girls get in the truck. I'm going to chase Outlaw out the back door."

"Run to the truck," I yell at Maggie and Rachel, even as I race around the side of the schoolhouse. I pull on the wooden door, and as it squeaks open, the sounds of the fight inside cause me to sob. How can Roxie survive a battle with Outlaw?

"Run, Jess," Cole yells, and I sprint back to the front of the building. Cole no longer bars the door, so I open it to see him raise the pointer Rachel had been waving.

He cracks it down on Outlaw's back, and now the cougar is distracted from Roxie. By Cole.

"No!" I think I scream the word, but I never hear it, so maybe it's in my mind. Or in my heart.

Outlaw leaves Roxie unmoving and turns that single eye on Cole.

Cole yells, "Get out!" and for a minute, I believe he means me. But he raises the thicker end of the pointer and slams it down on Outlaw's head. The unearthly screech of the cougar raises the hair on my neck, and I back away, unsure what to do. I want to grab Cole and pull him through the door, but I don't dare distract him. Outlaw would be on him in a second.

Cole raises the pointer again and pokes it at Outlaw's head, then belly, pushing the animal back several feet. Outlaw shrieks again, and the sight of that enormous mouth open and ready to tear Cole apart makes my knees buckle.

Then Outlaw pounces.

And so does Roxie.

She grabs Outlaw's leg as he lunges and gives such a yank that the cougar slams into the floor. He stands up, shaking his head, dazed. Then he staggers, and Roxie snaps at his other leg.

Outlaw yelps, this time in pain, and swings around toward Roxie, but Cole swings the pointer one more time, cracking it across the cougar's head. Outlaw falls, rises, and turns to stumble out the back door.

Cole runs over to close the door, then races back to where I stand, shaking and crying.

"Jess." Cole's words sound strangled. "Here are my keys. Drive the pickup to the steps so we can get Roxie up in the back. I'll call Doc Anderson and let him know we're on our way to the clinic."

I sprint to the pickup and start the engine, thankful for the hours of driving practice I had in this vehicle. Then, swinging the truck wide, I drive the 200 yards to where Cole waits, Roxie in his arms.

"Stay inside," I tell the girls, turning off the engine, then I leap out to help Cole.

Roxie is heavy, and we need several minutes to hoist her into the bed of the truck, being careful not to cause any more injury. She gives a sharp yip, and my heart hurts for her. Cole's mouth is a taut line, and I notice the strain in his face, not just from the weight of his dog but the fear for her life. Tears burn my eyes, but I can't swipe at them without dropping Roxie.

A rolled-up tarp lays in one corner, and we use that to cushion her. Cole sits down beside her and cradles her head on his lap.

He looks up at me, and the tears in his eyes mirror my own. "Let's go." He forces the phrase out in a thick voice, and I hop down, raise the tailgate, then slam it closed.

As I hurry to the front of the pickup, a tapping noise catches my attention. I look up to see Maggie and Rachel on their knees in the cab. They're pounding on the window, frantically gesturing at something behind me.

I round to see Outlaw watching us from the corner of the schoolhouse. Stifling a scream, I race to open the truck door, but my fingers slip, and I grab at it again. Then I yank the door wide and hurl myself inside.

"Buckle up," I say to the girls, but they appear mesmerized by the sight of the cougar and don't move.

"Now!" I summon my sternest voice, and they scramble around to find the seat belts. I switch on the key, and as soon as the second belt clicks, we are off.

The jerk of the truck throws us back against the headrests, and I peek over my shoulder to check if Outlaw has moved. He's pacing back and forth in the dirt. We're too far away, but I'm sure I can pick up the rumble of his growl.

"Maggie, slide open the rear window so I can talk to Cole," I direct, swinging the truck onto the one-lane road that will lead us back down the mountain. We'll have at least eight miles of this route before reaching a paved two-lane highway. The posted speed limit is 25 miles per hour because the road is so narrow.

"Jess!" Rachel screams, and I turn around, swerving dangerously near the edge of the lane.

"Look!" Both girls are pointing, and I glance in the rear-view mirror. For a minute, fear pools in my stomach as Outlaw stalks closer.

"Jess." Cole's calm—how can he sound calm—voice calls from the bed of the pickup.

"You might want to speed up."

"Ya' think?" I slam my foot on the gas pedal, and we lurch away.

"Oh no!" Maggie's cry draws my attention, and I glance over to discover her sitting halfway up on the bench, staring through the open back window.

"Down, Maggie," I order, but she doesn't respond.

"The tailgate is open," Rachel explains as she attempts to tug Maggie back into her seat.

I flash to the moment I closed the tailgate. I tried not to startle Roxie with a loud slam, but apparently, the lock didn't catch. The momentum of our takeoff over the bumpy road must have jarred it loose.

I risk a glimpse at the mirror and see Outlaw pick up the pace, causally loping closer. With the tailgate open, he only needs a little more momentum, a thrust from those powerful legs, and Outlaw will be in the truck bed with Cole and Roxie.

My sweat-slicked hands slip off the steering wheel, and I rush to secure my grip.

"Hold on." As I increase our speed, I realize with dismay that Outlaw is doing the same.

"Forty miles per hour. Cougars can run 40 mph." True North's words echo in my mind.

The speedometer shows we are traveling at a sedate 30 mph. If we were on a regular highway, I could pull away. However, this winding mountain trail doesn't allow speed. But with Outlaw gaining on us, I have no option. With each hairpin curve, I risk either running us into a tree or meeting another car for a head-on collision.

"God, please help." I'm not aware I spoke out loud until Rachel and Maggie add their prayers too.

In the back, Cole is shouting at Outlaw, trying to intimidate the powerful cat. But my next glance in the mirror shows the cougar is approaching the open tailgate.

One leap is all it will take.

I shift between watching the road and watching Outlaw, anticipating the moment his powerful muscles bunch, preparing to attack.

As I slam the accelerator down as hard as possible, I pray there is no car around the bend. For a minute, nothing happens. We continue our 30-mph pace even though my foot is pushing the gas pedal to the floorboard.

The cat lunges. Screams sound in my ears, and I recognize they are mine, mingled with those of Maggie and Rachel.

And in the next moment, the truck gives a tremendous shudder and hurtles away. The mirror reveals the shock in Outlaw's eye as he misses his target and comes down hard, catching his chin on the open tailgate.

He falls and lays still for a moment as we race away. I glance back to watch him stand to his feet, waiver and stagger. Then he takes wobbly steps and paces again. Maybe he's trying to decide whether we are worth the trouble.

I don't dare slow down, in case he gets a second wind, but soon we reach another turn, and I can't see him anymore.

I don't know if he is still chasing us or not, but I'm not

taking a chance. So instead, I focus my attention forward and call out to Cole. "Are you okay back there?"

"Yes," is his terse reply. I sense he wants to say, "Drive faster," but he won't. I've only had my license for a few weeks, and this type of driving is far out of my experience. Now that the cougar isn't a threat, we need to concentrate on keeping us all alive.

Another turn approaches, and I tap the brakes, slowing a little.

A swift glance in the mirror shows no stalking cougar, and I gulp in deep breaths.

Roxie whimpers, and while it breaks my heart to know she's hurt, the sound assures me she is alive.

For now.

19

I t's silent except for an occasional muffled sob from the girls. I can relate. There is nothing I'd like better right now than to stop driving, lay my head on the steering wheel, and howl.

But I must deliver Roxie to the clinic fast. I'll cry later.

Doc Anderson is waiting when I pull into the clinic's driveway. He vaults into the truck bed, and I watch through the back window as he examines Roxie, his usually smiling mouth set in a tight, grim line.

"Let's bring her inside," he says to Cole, and I hop out to open the door as they carry Roxie into the clinic. They disappear into an exam room, and I return to join Maggie and Rachel.

"Is Roxie alive?" Maggie's teeth chatter around the words.

"She is," I say. I don't add that she might not be for much longer. Maggie is a smart girl. She already knows that.

"Roxie saved our lives," Maggie whispers. Then she breaks. She turns in the seat and crawls into my lap, wrapping her arms around my middle. Her cries join Rachel's, and in a moment, we're a sobbing trio.

Scenes replay in my mind as we cry. I remember Maggie's face when we first walked into the schoolroom, her determination as she stood, eraser raised, ready to fight Outlaw.

My heart races at the memory of Cole shutting himself in with Roxie and Outlaw. To protect us. Roxie isn't the only hero.

Cole finds us huddled in the truck. He's exchanged his bloody shirt for a Beaverhead Animal Clinic T-shirt. At some point, I must have moved between Maggie and Rachel because both girls curl around me like puppies.

When I notice Cole approaching, I sit up, jostling the dozing girls.

I climb over Maggie, open the cab door, and hop down to join Cole. I try to speak but nothing comes out.

"Roxie is in surgery, but Doc can't make any promises." Cole's eyes are red-rimmed, and I can only imagine how difficult it must be for him to see her in such pain.

"She has multiple puncture wounds and has lost a lot of blood. Doc says the fact that she's young and strong may help her chances of survival." Cole's voice cracks on the last word, and I wrap my arms around him, giving and receiving comfort.

A few moments later, Cole pulls away. "I'm staying overnight. I called Nick, and he'll bring me clothes and food. He also said he'd let Sly know why you are running late."

"Oh no." I bite my lip. "I forgot to call her. She must have worried when everyone else came back but us."

"Nick and Sly were at the church to pick up the girls, still assuming they were riding with Jacquie. When they heard we'd gone back to find them, they drove home to wait. Nick was leaving for Bannack to check on us when I called him."

Startled, I ask, "Did you say Nick and Sly? Together?"

Cole nods. "Yes, I didn't have time to get any details from Nick, but they're together. At least at the moment."

I glance at my bag where my phone lives. "I bet I have tons of messages from Sly."

"A few," Cole agrees, and his attempt at a smile tugs my heart.

"Please call me when Roxie is out of surgery." I hate to leave him, but I need to take Maggie and Rachel home.

"Promise," he says, pulling me close for another quick hug. "Jess, you did a great job getting us down the mountain. I'm proud of you." He rests his chin on the top of my head, and we stand like that for a few seconds.

With a sigh, Cole steps back and glances at the clinic door. Then he strokes my cheek with his thumb, and I nuzzle against his hand.

"Go," I whisper. "She'll need to hear your voice when she wakes up."

He gives a brief nod and walks away.

I climb into the cab and look over at Maggie and Rachel, who watch me with wide eyes.

"Is Roxie going to die?" Rachel's voice is thin and wobbly.

"I don't know," I answer. "Outlaw hurt her, but Doc is doing everything he can to save her."

"I don't understand," Maggie flares. "True North said he killed Outlaw. Did he lie?"

Another question with no answer. I remember my suspicions the day True said he killed the cougar. Something seemed off, but it never occurred to me Outlaw was still alive. I thought another hunter fired the shot, and True took credit because of his vendetta. But why would he lie and put us all at risk?

As I pull onto the highway, my jaw tenses at the memory of my little sister and Rachel facing Outlaw in the schoolhouse. What if we hadn't arrived in time? We might have walked into a worse nightmare.

"How long were you in the schoolhouse with Outlaw?" I'm surprised the question hasn't occurred to me before now.

"Forever," Rachel says, and Maggie nods.

"We were writing on the chalkboard when we heard cars leaving the parking lot. That's when I realized I forgot to tell you we were riding back with you and Cole." Maggie sends me a guilty look. "We turned around to see Outlaw nudging open the front door."

Rachel reaches for Maggie's hand as they seem to remember their shared terror.

"He just watched us." Rachel takes up the story. "It was like he was waiting for ..." She shrugs and glances at Maggie for help.

"He was waiting for you and Cole. And Roxie." Maggie's voice cracks, but she continues. "He never came near us, but if we moved, he would growl and start pacing again."

I shudder when I consider the girls may have spent at least fifteen long minutes trapped by Outlaw. No wonder they said it was 'forever.' I'll always be grateful he didn't attack them, but I'm puzzled, too. Was Outlaw waiting for us? For Roxie?

There's no question Roxie saved the girls. She saved us all. Now she is fighting for her life because True North lied. I shake my head at the irony. True lied.

Now it's time to find out why.

<hr>

6:30 p.m.

A CROWD IS WAITING at the church parking lot when we arrive. Rachel's parents and brother hop out of their car when they see me park Cole's truck.

In seconds, friends and family surround us, anxious to know what happened.

Jacquie reaches me first, tears streaming down her face. "I'm so sorry," she repeats.

Maggie and I hug her. "Jacquie, it's not your fault." I begin.

But Maggie surprises me when she says, "Jacquie, please forgive me. I forgot to tell Jess that Rachel and I wanted to ride home with her and Cole. I'm sorry."

Jacquie, Maggie, and Rachel hug and cry as Sly hurries up.

"Blood." Tension fills her voice. "You have blood on your shirt."

"It's not mine," I assure her. "It's Roxie's."

Sly's eyes widen as she understands the significance.

Nick hurries over and asks, "Is Roxie out of surgery? Is Cole okay?"

"There's no word yet on the surgery. Cole isn't physically hurt, but ..." My voice breaks and Sly puts an arm around me.

"We've been praying while we waited for you," she assures me.

"Thank you," I say, and I'm surprised at how much peace settles over me. Somehow in the day's trauma, I almost forgot the most important part.

But God.

Maggie joins us, waving goodbye to Rachel. "Sly, it was awful. First, Roxie and Cole fought the cougar. Then Jess drove us down the mountain with Outlaw chasing us. It was like a movie."

"Hopefully with a happy ending." Nick gives Maggie a quick hug.

She hugs him back, then glances between Sly and Nick, puzzled.

"I thought," she begins, but Sly cuts her off.

"That's a story for another day. Let's take you two home."

Nick touches Sly's shoulder, and she turns to him.

"I'm going to the clinic and check on Cole and Roxie," he says. Then his eyes turn cold.

"When Cole told me Outlaw was still alive, I called Sheriff Herman, and he's organizing the trackers now."

I shiver at the thought of anyone having to face Outlaw again. What if they never find him?

"Please, God," I whisper. "This has to end."

Nick's jaw clenches as he says, "And then I'm going to find True North and discuss what really happened when he supposedly shot Outlaw."

GRACE AND KELLEN are sitting on our porch swing when we arrive home. The sight of Grace breaks down the last of my defenses. After telling the story so many times, I've become detached from my emotions.

But this is Grace. I'm crying before I even reach the top step, and Grace meets me there. She guides me to the swing, which Kellen vacates.

Sly murmurs, "Give them a few," as she invites Kellen into the house.

We swing until my sobs turn to sniffles, then Grace says, "I wish I'd been there with you."

"No, don't say that!" I shake my head, and my braid gives up the fight, leaving my hair to tumble around my shoulders. "I'm glad you were far away. It was so terrifying. Grace, Roxie could die." My voice catches on the name, and fresh tears fall as the weighty words hang between us.

"I know." Grace doesn't protest or deny the possibility. She's wise like that. "But whatever happens, God will help us through it. He always does."

That same peace I felt earlier finds a deeper place inside me, and I nod. "Always."

Grace reaches into her pocket and removes a folded stack of tissues. "Here, mop up."

10:00 p.m.

I'M startled awake by my phone's vibration. I stare at it in confusion, wondering why I fell asleep with it in my hand.

"Jess, answer it." Grace insists. I shake my head to dislodge the sleep still clouding my brain as Grace, Kellen, and Sly watch me in anticipation. Then I remember. Roxie!

The phone vibrates again, and I touch the screen to answer and engage the speaker option.

"'Lo?" My voice sounds like I'm underwater.

Cole says, "Hi, sleepyhead."

Tension drains from me, and I practically drop the phone. Cole sounds normal. Tired, yes, but also relieved.

I clear my throat and try again. "Roxie?"

"She made it through the surgery. Doc says if there are no complications, she should make a full recovery."

My heart catches on that word *should*. I want Cole to say *will*. But I understand Doc can't make promises, only assessments. Prognosis. The word pops into my mind, and I wonder if it is one of Grace's calendar words.

"Jess? Are you there?"

"Yes." Just when I thought I'd used up all my tears for the month, here comes a fresh batch.

"Hey, don't cry. I want to be honest. Roxie has a lengthy recovery ahead of her. But the fact she made it through surgery is a step closer to having her home with us again."

Kellen and Grace move toward the front door, and Sly follows them onto the porch.

I take the phone off speaker and say, "What about you? Are you okay?" While Outlaw didn't injure Cole, the trauma is deep. Yes, trying to outrun Outlaw was terrifying for me. But Cole had been in the back holding Roxie, wondering if she would survive long enough to reach the clinic. Wondering if she was dying in his arms.

"I may have a few nightmares," Cole answers. "But if my girls are good, I'm good."

My girls. My heart races as I nibble my lip, trying to think of a reply to his words. But my fuzzy brain fails me, and I know as soon as we finish the call, I'll come up with a dozen responses full of deep meaning. I sigh.

"Get some sleep, Jess," Cole urges. "You were amazing today. You helped save Roxie."

"And you helped save Maggie and Rachel," I remind him.

A few days earlier, I'd teased Cole, asking him who would save him if the clinic walls fell.

"You will," he'd answered. *"And I'll save you right back."*

I'd never imagined we would keep those promises so soon.

20

Sunday, October 21
9:00 a.m.

I'm a zombie. Sly says it's an adrenaline crash after yesterday. I drink a big mug of black coffee as I get ready for church and tuck a box of Junior Mints into my purse. Besides coffee, chocolate is my favorite source of vitamin caffeine.

The worship band is loud and upbeat, and soon my energy returns, although I add a nap to my afternoon schedule. We've been invited to the McBride's for dinner after church, and I hope I don't fall asleep in my mashed potatoes.

As the service ends, I gather my purse and Bible, turning to leave. I'm surprised to see Cole standing near the exit, looking exhausted. He'd texted me earlier to say Roxie was doing well, although he hadn't slept much. But before I can go to him, he holds up his hand and mouths the words, "Wait a minute," as he walks toward the other exit.

My heart drops when Cole approaches Gwen Torres. I flash to the Sunday when Grace and I met Outlaw for the first time. He'd been talking to Gwen that morning too. But I'd never asked Cole what they discussed that day.

Gwen is twenty and only attends church when she is home for a school break from Missoula College. I'm surprised to see her again so soon. I try not to stare at them, but I guess I'm not successful because Grace startles me when she whispers in my ear, "Relax."

I flinch, now the opposite of relaxed, and frown at Grace. "I don't know what you mean."

"Right." She nods toward the corner where Cole and Gwen are deep in conversation. "Gwen is roommates with Sierra, Cole's cousin. I'm sure he's asking her about how Sierra is settling in at Missoula."

"How did you know that?"

"My parents are in a Bible study group with Mr. and Mrs. McBride. Last week, Malcolm mentioned how pleased they are that the girls are roommates."

"Hmm," is all I say, but I relax. I know Sierra is attending college in Missoula, so it makes sense that Cole's checking on her. I need to work on not being so jealous. I trust Cole, but sometimes I wonder why he is with me instead of some older, prettier girl. Like Gwen.

Cole must sense I'm watching him because he looks straight up at me. I don't have time to turn away, so I have an unobstructed view of his expression. His forehead wrinkles a little like it does when he's thinking hard. His mouth is a straight, tight line, not smiling.

Cole says something to Gwen, pats her on the arm, and walks toward us.

Before I can speak, he says, "I need to find Nick. I'll catch you at dinner." Then he walks away.

"What do you think that's about?" Grace asks.

"Nothing good," I say.

IT'S BEEN a few weeks since my sisters and I shared Sunday dinner with the McBride family. The savory fragrance of pot roast greets us when we enter the spacious, farm-style kitchen, and my stomach rumbles. I glance around to see if anyone heard, but only Maggie smirks at me.

In the hour since church, Cole must have shared his concern with Nick and Mr. McBride because all three are solemn as we sit down to eat. Even Mary McBride isn't her usual serene self. She's trying, though, since Merry Jean, Cole's five-year-old niece, is joining us for dinner. Her parents are out of town, so MJ is staying with her grandparents for the week.

Mr. McBride prays, "Father, bless this food and all of us gathered here. Thank you for your protection yesterday and continue to heal Roxie. Watch over our travelers and especially our sweet Sierra. In Jesus' name, Amen."

We say amen, then I send a startled glance at Cole, but he gives a slight shake of his head, nodding toward MJ. Of course, we can't discuss Sierra's problem in front of the little girl. Cole's cousin is a year older than he is, and while I don't see her often, I always enjoy spending time with her when she visits Cole's family. Sierra is quiet and sweet, and I hate to think of anything bad happening to her.

Over dinner, Cole, Maggie, and I recount yesterday's adventure, trying not to alarm MJ. Her brown eyes fill with tears when Cole talks about Roxie.

When we finish the meal, Mary McBride says, "Maggie, would you be willing to take MJ to the family room and play a game for a little while?"

Maggie nods. I can tell she wishes she could stay to hear the conversation, but she enjoys playing games with MJ, so they hurry off.

As soon as they disappear, Nick says, "I found True and asked him why he lied."

I sit forward, not wanting to miss a word of this explanation.

"True said he didn't want anyone else to kill Outlaw. He hates the cougar for killing his dog, Pepper, and for the scar he carries because of Outlaw's attack. He says he deserves to be the one to end Outlaw's life."

"So, he was willing to put other's lives at risk for that reason?" Sly asks, outraged.

Nick shrugs. "Looks like. True said he never found Outlaw that day. So, he made up the story about chasing the cougar to a cliff and watching him fall to his death. He figured if everyone thought Outlaw was dead, they would stop hunting, and True could finish the job alone."

"But he didn't." Mr. McBride says grimly. "Instead, he left our children and pets vulnerable to more attacks."

"So, what happens now?" Cole asks. "Is True still hunting Outlaw?"

"We can't stop him," Nick answers, frustration clear in his voice. "But Sheriff Herman called in another outfit from Missoula. They should start the hunt later today. With the wounds that Roxie inflicted on Outlaw, it should be easy to locate him."

"I hate to think about killing any animal," Mary McBride says. "But that cougar caused so much fear and heartache. There is no other option."

"Plus, we should learn as soon as possible if Outlaw is infected with rabies, so we can identify if Roxie is at risk." Cole adds.

We're quiet as we think about Cole's brave dog and what we nearly lost yesterday.

"The next item of concern is Sierra." Mr. McBride says. "She's been having problems adjusting to college life, and she may be spending time with people who don't have her best interests at heart."

Mary McBride says, "Malcolm's sister, Connie, told me Sierra seldom answers her calls or texts, and last week she didn't come home for the weekend visit they had planned. Connie was ready to call the campus police to search for Sierra when she contacted her mother late Saturday night. Sierra said she forgot about the plans, and she had gone with some friends for a weekend in Butte."

"I haven't seen Sierra since she and Aunt Connie visited during spring break. But she was excited about starting college and studying to become a teacher. Did that change?" Cole asks.

"Yes, and it was a quick change," Mary agrees. "She started school at the beginning of August, and by September, she was ignoring Connie's calls. When they talk, Sierra only wants to discuss her plans with her new friends. She rarely mentions her classes or projects. Connie is worried." Mary McBride's beautiful eyes are dark with concern.

Nick says, "I contacted the campus police this morning after Aunt Connie spoke to Mom, and they called me about an hour ago. They found Sierra, but she was belligerent and angry. She said she's an adult and demands to be left alone to make her own choices."

"Jess, when Sierra visited in the past, you two were friendly." Malcolm McBride turns to me. "Has she reached out to you?"

I shake my head. "I texted her several times since she started school, asking how she liked it. The first time, in August, she answered and said she was enjoying the campus and classes. But a few weeks later, I texted again, and she never answered. So, I tried once more, but I figured she was busy with classes, and I didn't reach out anymore."

Mary sighs. "Yes, that's been my experience."

"I can try again," I offer, and Mary smiles.

"Thank you, but you're going through enough at the moment. Could I keep that option in reserve for later?"

"Of course," I agree.

"In the meantime, let's add our sweet Sierra to our prayers," Mary encourages us.

We are all quiet, and then Nick breaks the silence.

"In other news, I'm going to apply to be a special agent with the FBI." He lays his hand over Sly's, where it rests on the table.

Judging by her smile, this is not news to her. Mr. And Mrs. McBride also don't appear shocked, but Cole and I react together.

"What?"

Nick nods and continues, "While you two were playing Wild Kingdom yesterday, Sly and I had a lengthy, honest discussion. I explained the offer in the way I should have when I first told Sly about it on Tuesday."

He gives a rueful grin. "In my excitement, I forgot to explain that the application process takes a while. I can use that time to decide whether I want to pursue a career with the FBI or run for sheriff. If I move forward as a special agent, I'll have to complete the training and then request to be assigned a field office position in Missoula."

He gives Sly a smile that makes her blush. "That time will also allow Sly and me to learn where God is taking our relationship."

"That sounds like a wise plan," Malcolm McBride agrees while Mary McBride beams at them.

"The FBI," I say, allowing myself to be excited about the idea. When Sly told me about the offer earlier in the week, she'd been so brokenhearted I hadn't dared show any enthusiasm. But my brief encounter with the Missoula agents last month had made me very intrigued about what the FBI does. So now I'm eager to learn more through Nick.

Love shines in Sly's eyes as she watches Nick.

He turns to her, and the vulnerability in his gaze makes me look away. So, Nick *is* in love with my sister.

I give a slight smile and whisper, "Of course. What's not to love?"

"Did you say something, Jess?" Mary McBride asks, her deep brown eyes shining.

"Just happy words," I say, and she nods in understanding.

"There's one more thing we need to discuss." Nick's expression drains some of the happiness from me.

"Sheriff Herman and I spent considerable time going over the report of your parents' accident." He looks first at Sly, then me, and says, "We weren't able to find any evidence of foul play."

I protest, but Nick holds up his hand. "Wait, Jess. That doesn't mean there wasn't any, but it will be more challenging to prove it."

Sly is biting her lip, a sure sign she is trying not to cry.

But my reaction is anger. "Maybe your new FBI friends can help with that," I challenge.

Nick doesn't take offense at my tone but nods. "Could be," he says. "The FBI has the letter your dad wrote, and they're taking it seriously. I understand this isn't the news you wanted, but I promise I will continue to investigate."

Nick turns to Sly and repeats, "I promise."

"I know you will," she breathes, and the trust in her eyes overcomes my anger.

"I think we should pray together about the situation." Mr. McBride suggests. "Cole mentioned the other day that the BOB group has been discussing the difference between revenge and justice. God alone knows what happened that night, and He is the righteous judge. So, let's ask Him to bring justice, how and when He chooses."

Cole reaches out to take my hand as Mr. McBride leads us in prayer. I think of my words to Anthony Avery when I saw him last Tuesday.

"*I'm asking God for justice for my family.*" As we pray, I try to release my anger and need for revenge, giving God control.

As our amens echo around the table, Mr. McBride smiles and calls out, "Family meeting is adjourned."

"Yippee!" Maggie and MJ rush into the room, eager to join us again.

My heart skips at the word *family*. I gaze around the room, smiling as MJ launches herself into Cole's lap while Maggie leans over to whisper in Mary McBride's ear.

Mary smiles and gathers Maggie in a tight hug as Sly and Nick laugh with their heads leaned toward each other.

Family.

21

Monday, October 22
2:15 p.m.

"They caught him. They caught Outlaw!"

From behind me, the whispered words hit with a shock that nearly knocks me out of my chair. Across the aisle, Grace gasps. But before we can ask Martin Bellamy any questions, Madame Fellini turns from the whiteboard and confronts us.

Her brows draw together in a way that causes tiny lines to form above the bridge of her nose. They look like baby exclamation points.

"Mademoiselle Thomas, do you have something you wish to share with the class?"

I take a second to translate her question since we only speak French in class. I can feel my eyebrows mimic Madame's but stop when I remember wrinkles can start at any age. But it's unfair that I'm the one Madame focuses on, even though Martin and Grace were making more noise.

"No, Madame Fellini," I respond in my best French accent.

Unimpressed, she stares at me, then turns back and continues conjugating French verbs on the whiteboard.

Grace and I spin around to face Martin in sync, and I demand, "When?"

As Martin opens his mouth to respond, Madame Fellini twirls again.

"Mademoiselle Thomas, Mademoiselle Compton, eyes front, *s'il vous plaît.*"

I face forward, ignoring the snickers from the rest of the class. I peek at the clock, noting we still have thirty-two minutes left of French class, and I'm not positive I can stand the stress.

I consider asking for a bathroom pass, but the frown Madame gives me discourages that idea. Sighing, I settle in to endure the longest half hour of my life.

CHATTER FILLS the hallway with all kinds of information, none of it reliable.

"Outlaw attacked Sheriff Herman." The words float down the hallway, but when I turn, I can't identify the speaker.

"Naw, the cougar was already dead when they found him."

I swing around to question that report, but so many people are moving in the hallway I can't locate the source.

Once again, I'm frustrated that the upperclassmen are in the building across the street. I know Cole planned to check with Nick today while the trackers were chasing Outlaw. He'll have the facts.

As if my thoughts produce him, Cole arrives. Head and shoulders above the freshmen and sophomores, he makes his way upstream against the tide.

Several people try to stop him to talk, but he keeps moving toward me, although he shares a friendly smile.

Grace and Cole arrive at the same time, and he motions us toward an alcove.

"What happened?" The words burst from me.

"It's over. Outlaw is dead."

"For real this time?" Grace questions.

"Yes." Cole appears troubled, and I understand he hates that they killed an animal. Even one that nearly slaughtered Roxie.

"Did he," my voice cracks, and I try again. "Did Outlaw have rabies?"

"No." Cole's voice carries a depth of relief. "Now, we can focus on Roxie's recovery."

AFTER DINNER, I persuade Sly to let me spend time with Cole and Roxie. When I arrive, Doc explains he's concerned about the possibility of infection. He's shaved Roxie's silvery fur in places where angry red sutures cover her body. She's wearing a cone around her neck, which prevents her from biting her wounds. She's miserable but alive.

Doc has finished the autopsy on Outlaw, and he gives the report.

"Yep, he took a hard crack that broke his jaw. He dragged himself a mile or so off the road, but he must have died the same night he attacked our girl." Doc glances at Roxie with affection.

"It probably happened when Outlaw tried jumping into the truck bed," Cole explains. "The tailgate caught him under his chin."

I shudder, remembering the moment I saw the cougar charge toward Cole and Roxie.

"Thing is," Doc explains, "if the tailgate hadn't been down, it's unlikely Outlaw would have tried that jump. It would've been too high. He'd have given up the chase and wandered off to lick his wounds."

"And live to fight another day," Cole says.

"Yep." Doc picks up a giant flask of coffee and waves it at us.

I peer at my empty cup and shake my head. Doc's coffee is so strong I probably won't sleep until the weekend.

Cole nods his thanks, though, and I realize he plans to spend another night with Roxie. A cot sits in the corner, but it doesn't appear very comfortable. I doubt he'll sleep much, anyway. Thankfully, tomorrow is an in-service day at the high school, so we have no classes.

Doc continues. "Yep, it was fortunate the tailgate came down and lured the cat into taking that leap. Almost like a miracle."

I consider those words as I drive back to Justice. Almost like a miracle.

There's no almost about it, Doc.

I swing off the mountain road and onto the highway, passing Harvey's Lumber. A car leaves the parking lot and speeds up, pulling close to my back bumper. I increase my speed, but the driver continues to shorten the distance between us.

Unease ripples through me. I hate when someone follows too closely, so I speed up, hoping I don't get a ticket. But I don't want to be rear-ended either.

The headlights from an oncoming truck illuminate the interior of the car following me. I take a glance in my rear-view mirror and instantly recognize the driver.

Anthony Avery.

Instinctively I jerk on the steering wheel, and the Honda swerves toward the ditch. The tires slide on loose gravel, and I can hear my heart pounding in my ears. As I lift my foot to hit the brake, I realize that's the wrong choice. Cole's words echo in my mind, *"Take your foot off the accelerator and don't brake. Gently steer back onto the road."*

I resist the urge to look behind me. I can only deal with one crisis at a time.

The Honda enters the highway again, and I'm relieved to feel the pavement under my tires.

"Be calm," I speak into the silence surrounding me. "So,

Anthony Avery is driving behind me. He was probably at the lumber company for work. It's a coincidence I drove past as he was leaving." I peek in the mirror, glimpsing his shadowed face.

"Was he trying to run me off the road?" My eyes blur with tears. Is that how he killed my parents? It was raining; it wouldn't be difficult to cause them to crash.

Maybe Avery only meant it as a warning to my dad. But whatever his plan, my parents were dead as a result.

I shriek when Avery's bumper slams against mine. He's ramming my car! Irrationally I think, *'If I get a scratch on the Honda, Sly is going to kill me.'*

Unless Anthony Avery does the job first.

Another bump sends the Honda forward with a lurch. A moment before, several cars had been traveling this road, but now we're alone. I'm alone.

No, you aren't alone. I don't hear the words with my ears, but somehow, I understand them with my heart.

"God, please protect me," I whisper as another thump propels me forward.

An oncoming car passes, and I twist my head to show my terror-filled face. Of course, Avery slows until the vehicle passes, then he accelerates and rams into the Honda's corner. Once more, I skid toward the side of the road. Again, I hit the gravel and slide, but this time all four tires leave the road, and suddenly, I'm spinning.

The world twirls around, a kaleidoscope of trees, mountains, stars, and even a startled buck. But the deer is gone when I spin around again.

The Honda hurtles toward a wide growth of underbrush, then shudders and stops. I have one second to wonder if the airbag will deploy. It doesn't, and my forehead connects with the steering wheel. Dizziness and nausea come in waves. I close my eyes, trying to orient myself, then gather my courage and peek behind me where Anthony Avery's car had been.

He's disappeared. I face forward again, and in the distance, I see the red tail lights of his car speeding away.

Then everything goes dark.

"WE'VE GOT to quit meeting like this." The words are light, but the EMT's concern is obvious.

I'm lying on a gurney in an ambulance. We're driving fast, and the siren is giving me a headache.

"Let me check you over," The EMT's name tag reads Carl, and I recognize him from my last car accident, the terrifying ride with Mark last month.

"Do you have pain anywhere?" Carl asks. "The couple who called 911 said you were unconscious when they reached your car. They only saw the taillights of another car speeding away."

"I think I fainted," I say, doing an inventory of any physical injuries. None detected.

"Hey, no shame in that," Carl assures me. "Being run off the road is no fun for anyone. Well," he qualifies, "maybe for the runner."

"Not so much for the runnee," I agree.

The ER is quiet tonight, and I'm relieved to have the doctor's all-clear before Nick and Sly arrive. I assume they alerted Nick through the sheriff's department scanner since I'm sure I didn't make any phone calls. At least none I can remember.

"Sly, I'm sorry about the car." I don't give her a chance to say a word before I begin the apology.

"I'm so glad you're not hurt." Sly is fighting tears.

"The Honda is fine too," Nick says. "You slid on the gravel when you lost control of the car, but at least you didn't hit anything."

I frown. "Wait a minute, what do you mean I didn't hit anything? He hit me!"

Nick is doubtful. "Pete Davis didn't mention any damage. So, who do you think hit you?"

"I don't think, I know." I'm vehement. "Anthony Avery tried to kill me tonight."

22

By the time Nick drops us at home, I'm drooping. Nick is heading over to the sheriff's department, where Deputy Pete has driven the Honda. As I describe what happened, Nick's mouth forms a tight line of anger.

"I'll check for the damage," Nick assures me. "With the SUV Avery drives, it wouldn't have taken much of a hit to send you spinning. If we're lucky, we might find some paint from his bumper, although that's unlikely since it's chrome. It would be helpful to find some usable evidence." He doesn't sound hopeful, and I realize the truth.

I am the only evidence.

Now I settle on my bed, gathering my energy for a nice, hot shower. Sly is in her room, talking to Maggie, who is spending the night with Rachel.

"No, Jess is fine, Maggie." Sly's words are reassuring. "I wanted to tell you in case the Instagrammers started spreading the word. You stay with Rachel and enjoy your night; I promise Jess is fine."

I pick up my phone, debating whether I should tell Cole tonight or wait until the morning. He's so worried about Roxie; I hate to add more stress. Then I think, '*What if Cole had an accident and didn't tell you.*' In another second, I'm pushing his number.

"I was about to call you," Cole says. "Nick told me what happened. This is unreal. Are you okay?" Tears form at the concern in his voice, and I take a minute to respond.

"Jess?"

"I'm fine, no bumps, bruises, or contusions." But, of course, I don't mention the neck pain from being slammed forward and backward so quickly. A little ice should help that problem.

"This has to stop." Cole's sigh is deep. For a minute, I'm afraid he means us—that we have to stop. I want to explain I was not reckless this time, but before I can speak, he says, "Anthony Avery must be stopped."

I release the breath I didn't realize I was holding. "Nick is on it."

"Oh, I know he is," Cole says with dark satisfaction. "And this is one time my brother's stubbornness is a blessing."

10:00 a.m.

I'm so thankful we have no school today. I pace the kitchen, waiting for word from Nick.

"If you have that much nervous energy, why don't you go out and rake leaves or something?" Sly sits at the table, writing the updated article on True and Outlaw. I can tell she's anxious too, by the hunched tension in her shoulders.

By lunchtime, I've seriously annoyed Sly, who takes her laptop to her room.

I consider making dinner as a peace offering. I'm standing in front of the pantry, wondering if I should order pizza instead, when I hear a knock.

Nick! I hurry to the door and open it to see Grace.

"Oh." I try to hide my disappointment.

"I love you too." Grace breezes in, unoffended. We've been texting all morning, so she understands how eager I am to see Nick.

In the kitchen, Grace eyes the assorted boxes and cans I pulled from the pantry.

"Dinner," I explain.

"Uh-huh." She's skeptical.

Grace opens the fridge and rustles around, then says, "Yes!" in a tone I usually reserve for cheesecake.

She emerges holding a hefty package of chicken thighs. "Do you have a special plan for these?" she asks.

"Got me." I shrug. "Sly said they were on sale, so she grabbed them at the store yesterday. Why?"

Grace moves to the sink, opens the package, and cleans the chicken. Since that is one of my most hated jobs, I leave her to it.

"What can I do?"

"You can put everything back in the cabinet except the big bottle of salsa," she directs.

Mission accomplished, I return and watch Grace lay the chicken thighs on several paper towels to dry. Before I can ask for my next assignment, she says, "I think Crockpot liners are in that drawer near the stove."

I go to grab the liners, grateful Grace knows my kitchen even better than I do. Scrambled eggs are pretty much my only culinary accomplishment.

I line the Crockpot, then Grace places the chicken inside and dumps the entire jar of salsa on top. She replaces the lid, sets the timer for 6 hours on low, then turns.

"Voila. Salsa chicken. Serve it over rice with some shredded cheese. You can add sour cream if you prefer too. Delicious."

"Well, aren't you a regular Ree Drummond," I tease, mentioning Sly's favorite television chef.

"I wish." Grace returns to the sink and wipes down the counter with antibacterial soap.

"What's next?" she asks.

I'm about to suggest she bake some brownies when we hear a knock. Together, we say, "Nick," and race to the front door.

Throwing it open, I see not only Nick but also Cole standing there.

I invite them in, and Nick says, "We have news. Is Sly here?"

"Upstairs," I say, and Grace races to get her.

We take seats in the living room, and Cole squeezes my hand when he sits beside me.

Nick occupies my dad's recliner, but when I open my mouth to ask a question, he shakes his head. "Let's wait."

When Sly and Grace hurry into the room, Nick wastes no time getting to the point. "The FBI arrested Anthony Avery."

"For trying to hurt Jess?" Sly asks.

"For that, yes, and for much more." Nick's voice holds such satisfaction that my heart pounds.

"First, we found paint on the front of his company car. Then, we tracked him to an auto body shop where he was removing the evidence. This all happened last night."

Nick continues, "Early this morning, the sheriff's department and the FBI executed a warrant on his home, office, and car. The FBI has suspected Avery's involvement in fraud through his position as the Beaverhead County Building Inspector, as your dad's letter suggested. But they had no basis for a warrant. Until he tried to hurt Jess."

"We hit the jackpot with the warrant. Like Robert Sinclair, Avery kept a lot of incriminating information in his files. So, the FBI has more agents focusing on his crimes. They're charging him with attempted murder on Jess. Of course, his lawyer will ask for reckless endangerment instead. But there's extensive evidence to examine. It will take time before they can charge him in your parents' deaths."

I'm numb.

Sly's voice trembles when she asks, "Will Jess need to testify about what happened last night?"

Nick sighs. "I'm not saying this will be easy. Avery hired a high-priced attorney from Bozeman who fights dirty. But," he continues, seeing our concern, "it's also possible the district attorney will offer Avery a deal if he details other people's involvement in this crime ring. If that happens, there won't be a trial, and Jess won't need to testify."

"You mean Avery could go free, even though he murdered Daddy and Mamma?" I exclaim.

"Absolutely not." Nick shakes his head. "His cooperation might allow for a shorter sentence or a less restrictive facility. But Anthony Avery will be in prison for many years."

"Something's been bothering me," I say. "Why did Robert Sinclair have Daddy's letter in the first place? Daddy sent it to his boss, so why didn't he investigate a year ago?"

"I wondered the same thing," Nick admits. "Last week, the FBI asked Robert Sinclair that exact question, but he refused to answer. So, they assumed he was more scared of Avery than the FBI. But when the agents told Sinclair about Avery's arrest this morning, he suddenly had a lot to say."

Nick removes a little notebook from his shirt pocket and flips it open. "As we suspected, Sinclair and Avery were working together for some time. Plus, others may be involved.

When Avery realized Brian Thomas was getting suspicious, he made Sinclair install a program to intercept Brian's emails. It blocked anything addressed to employees of The Beaverhead County Building Inspector's office.

Sinclair read them, and if nothing suggested Avery was dirty, he sent them on, making it appear like he didn't intercept them. However, when he read the letter Brian sent to the Inspector's office, he contacted Avery. And of course, that letter never made it past Sinclair and Avery."

Nick continues. "Sinclair insists he had no idea Avery was going to do anything but try to intimidate Brian Thomas. He says it stunned him to hear about your parents' accident."

"Murder," I growl. "It was murder."

"What I can't understand is why Avery tried to hurt Jess last night?" Cole asks. "He had no reason, and it only brought the authorities into the situation. He's been careful, so what sent him over the edge?"

"Um, well, I may have an idea," I whisper. All eyes are on me now, and I gulp.

"Remember, Sly, when you asked me to take the ice cream freezer to Mrs. Irving last Tuesday? I, uh, ran into Anthony Avery outside the office that day."

"What?" Sly gapes at me. "Why didn't you tell me?"

I glance at Nick and back to Sly. "It wasn't a great day for you. I didn't want to upset you even more."

"Oh, Jess," Sly sighs. "I wish you had talked to me about it."

"What did you say to him?" Finally, Nick, the investigator, gets to the point.

I avoid everyone's eyes and focus on a spot over the bay window. A spider is spinning a web, and I make a mental note to move him later.

"Jess." Cole's voice is insistent.

I sigh, then confess, "I told him I had proof of what he did." So there, it's out.

Across from me, Grace gasps.

Sly asks, "What on earth were you thinking?"

"She wasn't," Nick growls.

Cole stands like I've ejected him from the couch. "You dared him to come after you," he clips.

"No." I hurry to stand beside him. I don't care if others are in the room. I need to make him understand. "That was not my intention," I say.

"Yes, I was angry. Avery said something about watching where I was going, or I might get hurt. Those were the exact words he said to Daddy. It sounded like a threat to me. He was just so smug, and I didn't want him to think he could escape forever."

"But I didn't taunt him to come after me." I touch Cole's arm, trying to communicate my sincerity.

"Maybe not, but that was the result, right?" He moves back, stepping away from me. From us. "I need to check on Roxie. We'll talk about this later."

I wonder if that's a threat or a promise. But then, a moment later, Cole's truck roars away.

Nick breaks the silence. "You scared him, Jess. Men don't like to be scared, so we sometimes react in anger. Give him time to process."

I nod miserably and say, "Thank you for everything you've done. Please let me know if I can answer any other questions."

Then I walk upstairs, lock myself in my room, and ugly cry.

5: 00 p.m.

I'M SITTING on the swing, feeling sorry for myself, when Maggie crosses the yard and joins me. Rachel had a dentist appointment, so Maggie spent a few hours with Mrs. Mendelssohn.

"Hey, Magpie," I greet her. "How was your afternoon with Mrs. M?" Maggie's color isn't great. In fact, she's a little green.

"Terrible." She flops beside me and pushes against the floor, sending the swing higher. "Mrs. M had a brand-new recipe she wanted me to help her make."

"Yes, I heard about that. Turtle pie, right? Did she use real turtles?"

"Ha," Maggie says, with no humor in her voice. "No turtles

were harmed in the making of the pie. It's chocolate and fantastic. Especially for Mrs. M."

"She gave me a piece when I got there today, but I think she used it to ... I don't know ..." Maggie's brow wrinkles as she searches for the words.

"Lure you into a false sense of security?" I suggest with a smile.

"Exactly." Maggie shakes her head at Mrs. M.'s deception.

"So, what did you make?"

"Quiche."

"Well, that's not too bad. In fact, I like quiche."

Maggie eyes me with close to malicious intent. "Why don't you go over and ask for a sample?" she says, and her sweet smile makes me nervous.

"What was in this quiche?" I ask suspiciously.

"Liver and onions."

My earlier lunch is on the verge of reappearing as I imagine the smells that must have filled Mrs. M's kitchen all afternoon. I lean over to sniff Maggie. "Shower," I say.

"No kidding," she says as she vaults from the swing. But unfortunately, the rocking sensation that follows doesn't settle my stomach.

Poor, traumatized Maggie. At least we have salsa chicken for dinner.

Grace was right. The meal is delicious—at least Sly and Maggie think so. I eat a little but don't taste it.

After dinner, Sly nudges me toward the door. "You cooked, Maggie, and I will clean."

I give a shaky smile. "I put in a Crockpot liner."

"You brought Grace into our lives. I'll give you extra credit for that. "

I wander to the porch and settle onto the swing. Someone left a warm blanket on the seat, anticipating the cooler weather. I gather it around me and start the slow motion of the swing.

I close my eyes and try to push away the swirling thoughts in my mind. Anthony Avery is going to prison. Nick might become a special agent with the FBI. Outlaw is gone, but Roxie still faces a lengthy recovery. And Cole's mad at me. Again.

The creak of the wooden steps startles me, and I open my eyes to see Cole.

"I didn't hear your truck."

He shrugs. "I left it at my house. I needed the walk."

Nibbling my lip, I ask, "Do you want to sit down?" I scoot over, bunching the blanket around me.

I offer him a corner, but he shakes his head and tucks it more closely around my shoulders.

"I'm not cold," he says, and somehow, I know that's true. He was cold this afternoon when he walked out of the house. But that harshness has faded from his face.

"I'm sorry," I whisper.

"Me too."

We swing for a few minutes, then he says, "Sometimes you scare me."

I surprise us both with a laugh. "Sometimes, I scare myself."

His lips twitch, but he continues to gaze forward, seeing something I can't.

"I'm worried about Roxie."

"Me too," I repeat his words from earlier. "Do you remember when we sat on this swing last month? Sly was facing possible jail time, which would put Maggie and me in foster care."

He turns to me. "I remember. We prayed."

"We prayed," I agree, reaching for his hand. "Let's do that again."

Afterward Cole says, "You should go inside. You're shivering."

I stand, still wrapped in the blanket. "I don't want you to leave yet."

"I don't want to go," he says. "But I need some sleep. That cot at the clinic is brutal. Plus, classes start again tomorrow."

"Ugh, don't remind me."

"Tell you what. After BOB tomorrow, we'll go visit Roxie for few minutes."

"I'd like that," I agree.

Cole wraps his arms around my mummified self and pulls me close. Despite the chill, his nearness warms me, and then so does his kiss.

After a minute, he steps away and smiles.

"Sweet dreams," he says, his gray eyes sparkling even in the darkness.

I watch as his long strides take him toward his home.

Then I go inside and have those sweet dreams.

23

Sunday, November 4
6:30 p.m.

Family. I grasp the photo album and gingerly turn the page, almost as if I'm afraid of what I'll see. But there are no surprises. I've studied this album front to back many times. One night I even fell asleep with it open on the bed, my hand resting on my favorite picture of Daddy and Mamma.

Today is hard. I knew it would be, but anticipating and experiencing are two different things. This morning, we went to church, my sisters and I, alternately wanting to be left alone and craving the comforting hugs from our friends. Afterward, Sly drove us directly to the cemetery, where we placed new flowers on Daddy and Mamma's graves.

They've been gone a year. While it seems like a second, it also seems like a lifetime. We cried a lot today. And we also laughed as we took out some cherished memories and looked at them in a new light.

"Sly, remember the first time you cooked a full meal by yourself? You coated the chicken tenders in powdered sugar instead of flour." I say.

"Hey, I was only 11," Sly defends herself. "Poor Daddy, I can still see the look on his face when he took his first bite."

"How about the time Mr. Bailey's goat, Henry, got loose and started eating Mamma's zinnias? She grabbed her broom and chased him all the way home." Maggie adds her favorite.

"Daddy was driving down the street and saw her running after Henry. He started laughing so hard he had to pull over." This time Sly's tears are caused by laughter.

We gather close together on the couch with Sly in the middle. I hand her the album, and we spend precious time remembering the love our parents gave us.

Wednesday, November 7
6:30 p.m.

"SURPRISE!" As Cole and I enter Pastor Jarrod and Anna's home, Caleb leads the BOB group in the chorus of "Happy Birthday."

I display my best Oh-wow-I'm-so-surprised look, and Grace gives me a grin and thumbs up. She told me about the party last night.

"I know it's supposed to be a surprise." Grace had stopped by after dinner to give me the heads-up. "But I just wanted to make sure it was okay with you, considering the timing ..." Her voice had trailed off as she watched me in concern.

I wasn't sure what touched me more. That the BOB group wanted to throw me a surprise party or that Grace was so sensitive to my feelings she was willing to share the secret in case I wasn't ready.

Last year there had been no birthday party. The "Sweet 16" banner Mamma had ordered was packed away, in safe keeping for when Maggie could use it. We'd buried our parents the day before, and just the thought of a celebration made me physically ill.

But now, finally, I'm ready.

The song ends, and suddenly I'm surrounded by my friends and family. Sly and Nick are there, along with Maggie and Rachel.

And Cole. I touch the thin leather bracelet he gave me earlier tonight. It is sturdy and delicate, which seems like a contradiction but isn't. Etched into the leather is the word *BRAVE*.

"I know it doesn't always seem like it, but I do love your bravery." Cole said.

"Even when I take risks?" I teased.

"Even then." He kissed me so sweetly tears stung my eyes. He looked at me then and asked, "Are they happy or sad tears?"

"Happy," I said. "Only happy."

Now I look at the people I love so dearly, and somehow, I know. Seventeen is going to be a great year.

24

Saturday, November 10
1:00 p.m.

"They're here; they're here!"

MJ's voice carries above the chatter and laughter in the McBride kitchen.

Mary McBride straightens from the oven, where she's checking on the turkey. Sly switches off the electric mixer she's using to mash the potatoes. I step away from the table where I'm arranging Sly's homemade rolls on a tray.

We race from the kitchen, pouring onto the front yard to join the other adults. Maggie and MJ are hopping in excitement.

My heart speeds up as Cole's truck pulls into the driveway. The girls are quiet when they see that Cole appears to be alone.

Then Cole turns and says something I can't hear. Suddenly, our beloved Roxie is with us, barking and nuzzling MJ and Maggie as they kneel and carefully wrap their arms around her neck.

Everyone gathers around Roxie, but I hold back, watching from the porch. Cole glances up from the celebration, then joins me.

I answer his huge grin with one of my own.

"I'm so glad we're all here to welcome her home."

Several of Roxie's wounds became infected, and the last week has been a roller-coaster of emotions. Doc thought it was best to keep her at the clinic a little longer. She still faces more recovery and rehab, but she's getting stronger every day.

"Timing is everything," Cole agrees as he reaches out to pull me close. "Mmm, dinner smells great."

"Your mom outdid herself," I agree.

Since Cole's sister, Piper, her husband Jack, and MJ will be spending the holiday in Oregon with Jack's family, Mary McBride insisted on celebrating two Thanksgivings this year.

"This will be First Thanksgiving," Nick explains as he passes the gravy. "Then, in two weeks, we'll celebrate Second Thanksgiving."

"Kind of like the Hobbit's Second Breakfast?" Maggie asks.

"Exactly." Nick grins.

Later, as we sit around the dining table, full of turkey and dressing, Mr. McBride asks, "Will anyone share what they're thankful for this year?"

"I'm thankful for Grandma's pumpkin pie," MJ announces, eyeing the side table covered with a variety of desserts.

While each person takes a turn, I'm aware my throat is tightening. No, I can't cry now. But grief sneaks up on me as I think of how much Daddy and Mamma would have enjoyed this time together.

I glance around the table, searching for anything that will distract my thoughts. Between the green bean casserole and candied yams sits the special cranberry salad Sly made. It shimmers in Mamma's favorite crystal bowl.

For a moment, I consider excusing myself and leaving the table before my turn arrives. But Cole's hand reaches for mine, and his gentle squeeze steadies me.

"I wonder if it's First Thanksgiving in heaven?" Maggie's voice is soft, even with the weight of her words.

Everyone is quiet as they consider the question, then Nick leans over and gives Maggie a brief hug. "Magpie, I think in heaven, every day is Thanksgiving."

On his other side, Sly brushes a tear away and glances up, giving me a watery smile.

Healing, I think. *This is what healing looks like.*

THE AFTERNOON PASSES in an easy rhythm. Clean up is a family affair, and although we keep running into each other, that's part of the fun.

Later, Cole and I invite Nick and Sly to join us when we take Roxie for a walk. We pass a few neighbors who have the same idea, and greetings echo around us. I can smell snow in the air. Soon, it will cover Justice like a blanket. But for now, the sidewalks are dry, and we laugh together at Roxie's unbridled joy at her freedom.

Ahead of us, Sly and Nick laugh when he playfully tweaks the orange pom-pom on her knit cap. Her cheeks are glowing with cold and happiness. I wrap my arms around myself, wishing I could hold on to this moment forever.

"Cold?" Cole tugs me close, but I shake my head.

He seems to understand and reaches to smooth my hair back from my face. I'm wearing it down, and now Cole wraps one curl around his finger.

"So pretty," he says.

I'm expecting a kiss, but instead, Roxie gently nudges me.

"Hey." I look down at Roxie, who regards me with innocent eyes.

"Jealous much?" I whisper as I bend to rub behind her ears.

"C'mon, slackers," Nick calls out from ahead of us. "It's pie time."

The sun is setting when we return to the house, and my breath catches when I see the glowing candles in every window.

Cole chuckles. "Mom has enough batteries to keep them lit until February."

"She says people have used candles for years to welcome home a traveling family member," Nick adds.

"I love it," I say.

"It's so inviting," Sly whispers, and I expect soon our home will have candles in every window too.

We enter the warmth of the house and hang up our coats. Roxie lopes to the back porch and her water bowl while the rest of us discuss dessert.

We're in the middle of a game of Monopoly when the house phone rings. Mary jumps up to answer it, saying, "That will be my sister-in-law, Connie. She usually calls on Saturday night."

"Hi Connie," Mary answers with a smile. "Go ahead. You're on speaker."

But instead of Connie's voice, all we hear is a muffled sob.

"Aunt Mary?" The trembling voice is practically unrecognizable.

"Sierra?" Mary asks in concern. "Are you okay? Are you with the family?"

"No." The word is a wail. "Is Nick there?"

"I'm here, honey." Nick moves closer to the phone. "What's wrong? Where are you?"

For a moment, I worry the phone disconnected. Then Sierra whispers, "That's the problem. I don't know where I am. But I'm in a lot of trouble."

Nick motions for Cole to hand him his cell phone. "Sierra, what kind of phone are you using? I can track it if you give me the number." Nick writes a text, probably to the sheriff's department.

Sierra recites a number, urging, "Please hurry, Nick. I don't know when they might come back to move us."

"Who are *they*?" Nick shouts, then he attempts to calm himself. "How many? What do they look like? Have they said their names?"

Silence.

"Sierra? Are you there?"

But she's gone.

HOURS LATER, I sit with Sly on our love seat. Maggie is finally asleep, although her tender heart is breaking for Sierra and all the McBride family. So is mine.

"Look at me." I touch Sly's arm. "Sierra will be fine. Nick will be fine."

Sly nods, but I can see the worry, like a dark cloud, hovering over her head.

Nick and Malcolm McBride are driving through the night, headed to Missoula to search for Sierra.

"Sly, look at me," I repeat, and as she faces me, I wish I hadn't insisted. Her brown eyes are swimming with tears that threaten to spill down her cheeks.

I swallow hard. "Our families have been through so much. But God always makes a way for us. Always."

Sly nods and I see her shoulders relax.

I turn and raise my knee to settle onto the love seat and continue, "I'd hoped by now we could settle everything with Anthony Avery and Robert Sinclair."

"Me too," Sly says. "Today, Nick told me Avery's attorney is fighting every step of the way. So, we may have to wait months before we see justice."

"I used to think being a Christian meant nothing bad would ever happen to me," I admit. "But we know that's not true."

Sly nods. "I wish it were," she says in a small voice.

"But God promises to make all things work for good for those who love Him. That's us, Sly. And we've seen Him do it, over and over. That will not change, because God will not change."

"But God," she whispers, a tiny smile on her lips.

"But God," I agree, echoing our Mamma's favorite phrase.

"So, how'd you get to be so smart?" Sly leans over to give me a quick hug.

"I had some excellent teachers," I admit with a grin.

25

Sunday, November 11
6:30 a.m.

My eyes pop open, and I give an accusing glare at Tweety. But he sits in silence, and a moment later, I realize what woke me. A dog is barking outside my window. But not just any dog. Roxie.

I quickly pull back the curtains, revealing Cole and Roxie standing in the yard below my window.

Motioning Cole to the front, I grab my fuzzy pink robe and wrap it around my sweat pants and T-shirt. I give a fleeting thought to brushing my teeth, but I remember my stash of gum and dig in the robe's pocket.

My breath is minty fresh when I open the door to join Cole and Roxie.

"What's going on? Did Nick find Sierra?" I ask the questions as I protect myself from Roxie's exuberant greeting.

"No." That one word pierces my heart, and I walk to the swing on shaky legs.

Cole settles beside me and restlessly puts the swing in

motion. "Nick met with the campus and Missoula police, but they found no sign of Sierra. Aunt Connie had hoped she would call this weekend, but she didn't."

"She called Nick instead," I say, and Cole nods.

"Yes, I guess she thought Nick would be her best chance to be rescued. But, unfortunately, the phone she used was not traceable."

Cole sighs and reaches over to draw me closer. I'm not sure if it's for warmth or comfort, but I snuggle into him.

"Sierra isn't the only girl who has disappeared from campus," he says. "Another vanished this spring and is still missing. Plus, there are several others from the county and the reservations."

I close my eyes, steeling myself for what I suspect Cole will say next.

"A task force is being formed. They believe a trafficking ring is operating near Missoula. And they may have taken Sierra."

8:00 p.m.

Mary McBride paces her family room, and I wonder if there will be a permanent track in the carpet where she walks.

"Mom, by the time they arrive, you'll be exhausted. Please try to sit and relax." Cole urges Mary to the couch.

She perches there like a bird about to take flight. Tension fills the air, and Roxie gives a mournful whine. Cole reaches down to pat her with his left hand. His right hand is holding mine.

From the kitchen, I hear Sly and Maggie talking as they remove brownies from the oven. Baking is Sly's stress reliever. Unfortunately, eating is mine. It's a symbiotic relationship.

Roxie's ears perk up, giving us our first sign that Nick and Malcolm have returned. Mary launches herself across the room to welcome them home.

Nick and Malcolm. But not Sierra.

Nick stamps his feet to loosen the snow clinging to his boots. Then he steps inside and efficiently removes them and his Deputy's parka. Sly materializes by his side, looking relieved and sad at the same time.

Mary hurries to her husband, and he wraps his arms around her, resting his chin on the top of her dark head.

The questions start as everyone speaks at once. Nick holds up his hand in a gesture that reminds me of Cole and the birthday party. It works the same way, and everyone is quiet.

"We're on their trail," Nick says, getting down to business. "They're heading to Canada but moving slowly. They're probably stopping to pick up more girls."

Nick crosses to Mary. "Mom, the experts tell me they won't hurt the girls."

"No," she says bitterly. "They will sell them."

Nick nods. "That's their plan, but we have our own, and we're going to stop them. I promise."

I'm startled by the assurance in Nick's voice.

As if he read my mind, Cole murmurs, "Nick doesn't make promises he can't keep. He *will* find Sierra. He'll find them all."

As the men devour the leftovers Sly prepared for them, Nick outlines the task force's strategy. It's dangerous, and Nick has only returned long enough to recruit others to help.

"Sheriff Herman has agreed to let Levi Cooper go to Missoula with me to join the task force," Nick explains. "We're leaving tomorrow afternoon."

Nick and Malcolm finish the meal, and Sly stands to take the dishes to the kitchen. Nick follows, and I can hear their quiet murmurs as he reassures her.

"I called Rory Fletcher on the way home this evening, and he's agreed to take over my outstanding cases. I have a hearing before Judge Breen in the morning, then I will be free to travel with Nick and Levi," Malcolm McBride says, and Mary nods in agreement.

I can tell he's struggling with the idea of leaving his law

clients on such short notice, but he's just as determined as Nick to find Sierra.

I think about Sierra, with her shy smile and shining brown eyes, terrified and alone. I can still hear the fear in her voice when she told Nick, "I don't know where I am, but I'm in a lot of trouble."

It's been over two days since we heard her voice. What if the kidnappers are already on their way to Canada? What if the task force can't locate them and we never see Sierra again?

I hold my hands together tightly to keep them from trembling. My heart races as I imagine what might happen to Sierra—what might be happening right now.

But God. The words are so clear I look around to see who spoke, but no one is nearby.

"But God," I whisper in response.

ONE BY ONE, we all gather in the living room again. Cole takes his place beside me on the sofa, and I snuggle under his arm as he holds me close. Malcolm and Mary McBride settle into the loveseat as Maggie sits on the floor near their feet.

Sly and Nick return from the kitchen, and I can see my sister has been crying. My heart aches for her, knowing she's sending Nick into an unknown and dangerous situation.

As the darkness settles, I study the candles lighting the windows of the McBride home. Of course, our windows have candles too. Grace, Anna, and several others from Justice have put candles in their windows. It's a sign they are standing with us in prayer for God to bring Sierra home.

I gaze around the room at the people I love. Family.

The coming days will be challenging for all of us. We've already faced so much. But again, Mamma's words echo in my heart, and I settle in for the journey, knowing we won't be alone in the fight.

But God.

ABOUT DEBBI MIGIT

Debbi Migit lives in central Illinois, surrounded by pumpkin patches and corn fields. She has won multiple awards and contests, writing stories that are filled with faith and hope. She loves to share personal anecdotes about God's faithfulness, infusing her talks with authenticity and humor.

Her first book, Child of Promise, is the true love story of a family formed through adoption. After ten years of infertility, Debbi and her husband, Phil, were just months from adopting when God said, "Not this way." Child of Promise is the story of audacious faith resulting in multiple miracles; it encourages readers to remember their own promises and believe again.

Debbi and Phil are the adoptive parents of Alex, Ethan, and Kate. The God-ordained spacing of their children offered the unique opportunity to parent a teen and two toddlers at the same time. This is the season Debbi fondly calls the TNT years!

Debbi's hobbies include reading, writing, and avoiding arithmetic. Her favorite color is turquoise, and she collects Trixie Belden books and typewriters. If playing Candy Crush was a paying gig, she would be rich.

Debbi's new romance/suspense series begins with September Shadows, and is set in Montana. After the mysterious death of their parents, three young sisters are determined to stay together and make a new life for themselves. This new life includes faith-testing danger, adventure, and romance.

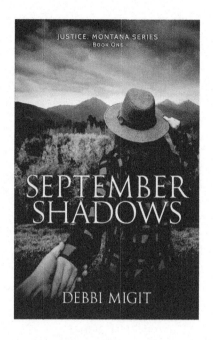

September Shadows

Book One - Justice, Montana Series

After the sudden death of their parents, Jess Thomas and her sisters, Sly and Maggie, start creating a new life for themselves. But when Sly is accused of a crime she didn't commit, the young sisters are threatened with separation through foster care. Jess is determined to prove Sly's innocence, even at the cost of her own life.

Cole McBride has been Jess's best friend since they were children. Now his feelings are deepening, just as Jess takes risks to protect her family. Can Cole convince Jess to trust him-and God-to help her?

NEXT IN THE JUSTICE, MONTANA SERIES

...

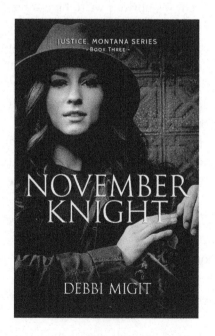

November Knight
Book Three - Justice, Montana Series
Coming October 2022

Here's a sneak peek at Chapter One of *November Knight*:

Monday, November 12
3:30 p.m.

"Jess, this isn't a good idea." My best friend, Grace, is breathless as she tries to keep up with me. I shorten my steps, realizing my attempt at a casual stroll has morphed into a power walk.

"You're right," I agree. "I was walking too fast. We need to act normal or we might look suspicious." Although Grace and I are both seventeen, it's obvious we're high-schoolers. I feel like we're wearing flashing signs that say, *Intruder Alert!*

Several college students are approaching on the sidewalk, and I grab Grace's arm, throwing my head back and laughing like she's said something hysterically funny.

To her credit, Grace goes along with the fake joke until the students pass, then she abruptly stops laughing.

"Yep, we don't seem suspicious at all." Her tone implies an eyeroll. "I meant, it's not a good idea to be here, on this campus. We need to let Nick do the investigating. He's the deputy sheriff, after all."

"Hmmm," I say, which translates into, '*I hear you, but I'm ignoring your advice.*'

"You're ignoring my advice, aren't you?" Grace asks.

"Hmmm."

"Well, at least I can tell everyone I tried to talk you out of it."

The resignation in her sigh tugs at my conscience, and I try to reassure her. "It's just a little bit of intelligence gathering. I can't stop thinking about Sierra's phone call to Nick on Saturday. Someone took her and we have no idea where she is. When Nick went to Missoula to search, he found out the police and FBI have been investigating a trafficking ring operating near the campus. He can't be sure they took Sierra, but it's a place to start. I have to do something to help find her."

"I'm confused," Grace continues. "If Sierra attends the University of Montana in Missoula, why are we looking for clues on the Dillon campus?"

"According to Nick, Sierra volunteered here at the Youth Challenge Program twice a month. Her roommate, Gwen Torres, assumed that's where she was going when she left their dorm on Friday afternoon. Sierra always stays with a friend, Naomi Crenshaw, when she's in Dillon."

"It sounds like Sierra has a big heart if she gives two weekends a month to help at-risk kids," Grace says thoughtfully. "But you said earlier she was skipping trips home to see her mom and not answering calls. I wonder why Sierra suddenly pulled away from her family and friends?"

"I don't know," I say. "Let's find her and ask."

As we turn a corner, a large, brick building looms in front of us. I infuse my tone with surprise and say, "Hey, look. There's Magnus Hall, where Naomi lives."

"Shocking."

I frown at Grace's tone. While sarcasm is pretty much my default setting, Grace usually is very trusting and sweet. But over the past few months, my 'adventures,' as I call them, seem to have sharpened Grace's edges more than a little.

Great, I've broken my best friend.

"C'mon," Grace's genuine smile eases my conscience. "Let's stop and see if Naomi is around."

I shake my head. "No, Naomi is at the sheriff's department in Justice, being interviewed by Nick and Levi."

"How'd you know that?" Grace asks, then laughs lightly. "Never mind, stupid question."

"There are no stupid questions," I quote our French teacher, Madame Fellini.

"Only stupid accents." Grace finishes the quote with a grin.

I stop walking and stare at the three-story brick building, suddenly doubting my plan. I thought while Naomi was busy at the sheriff's department, I could check her dorm for clues. I brought Grace along as a lookout, because, hey, what's a little breaking and entering between friends?

But the trusting expression on Grace's face makes me reconsider. I haven't even told her about her part in the plan, and now I feel guilty. I really hate feeling guilty.

"C'mon." I tug Grace's arm and turn us back in the direction of the student parking lot where I parked my sister Sly's car. "I don't know why I thought I could find Sierra by just walking around campus. She's been missing since at least Saturday. She could be in another state by now." I'm surprised when my voice cracks on those last words.

We climb into the Honda and sit in silence for a minute, then Grace says, "I'm scared."

"Me too."

"Does Nick have any clues at all?" Desperation laces her words.

Deputy Sheriff Nick McBride is Sierra's cousin and the one she called Saturday night. He is also Sly's boyfriend, while his younger brother, Cole, is my boyfriend. I guess we like to keep things in the family.

Sierra called during a family gathering which included the entire McBride and Thomas clans. Well, the McBrides are a clan. My sisters Sly, Maggie, and I are more of a clan-ette.

"Not really," I say. "Tomorrow, Nick and Levi are joining the task force in Missoula that's focused on finding the traffickers. Hopefully, they will have some new information that will bring Sierra home."

My throat tightens when I think of what Sierra might be facing right this minute. She must be terrified. I whisper the same prayer I've repeated many times since she called Nick three nights ago. "Please, God, keep Sierra safe and bring her home soon."

I glance at Grace and see tears trickling through the freckles that dust her cheeks.

"Hey," I say, reaching to touch her arm. "God's got this. We have to trust Him."

Grace swipes at the tears and nods.

"Since we're in Dillon, let's stop and see Verity," I suggest, hoping to lighten our moods.

"I'd like that." Grace agrees.

I turn the car in the direction of downtown Dillon to Verity's shop. Last month Grace took me to the specialty shop to look for accessories for our homecoming outfits. Grace had shopped there before, since she loves vintage jewelry and clothing. I was surprised to discover that Verity and my mom had been friends.

Since my parents' murder a year ago, I treasure every memory of them. So, when Verity shared some of the conversations she had with my mother, it made me feel like Mamma was right there with us, just for a few minutes.

The bell over Verity's door announces our arrival at her shop, and I stop for a moment to inhale the unique scent of the store. The spicy tang of apple cider, mixed with the sweet aroma of freshly baked snickerdoodle cookies, smells delicious.

Verity stands behind the antique table that serves as a sales counter. At the sound of the bell, she looks up and gives us a dazzling smile. Two women stand at the counter with their backs to us, and I notice they have a variety of items laid out on the table. I'm not sure if they are buying or selling, but I nudge Grace, and we head over to the cookie table to wait until Verity is free.

"Oh man," Grace mumbles around a mouthful of cookie. "These are amazing."

I lift the lid of the small crockpot and ladle hot apple cider into two paper cups, then hand one to Grace. She takes a sip, and her eyes widen.

"Delicious and ... spicy?" She peers into the cup. "I wonder what she added to the cider?"

I take a taste and grin. "Red Hots," I say. "That's how Mamma used to make cider too."

I sip again, close my eyes, and for a moment, I remember Mamma and Daddy in our kitchen discussing how many Red Hots to put into the cider.

"Brian," Mamma said, "The recipe calls for one cup of Red Hots, not one whole bag."

"If some is good, more is better." Daddy reached around her and tried to pour more of the spicy candy into the large pot on the stove.

I smile, remembering how Mamma waved her wooden spoon at him, shooing him away. Daddy had retreated, only to swoop back, kiss Mamma on the cheek, and drop a handful of candy into the pot.

My sweet memory is interrupted by the sound of raised voices.

"Uh-oh," Grace whispers. "It sounds like Verity is having some trouble."

"I know it's worth a lot more than that!" The duo at the counter have added more items to the pile they're trying to sell to Verity. "Look how shiny it is. It's probably pure gold."

Grace and I approach the table in time to see Verity reach into a drawer and pull out a large magnet.

"Let's check," she says with a tight smile. She picks up the gold-colored ring and touches it to the magnet where it attaches.

"I'm sorry," Verity says, kind but firm. "Gold is not magnetic, so this piece is actually gold-plated. It really is a pretty ring, and I'm sure I can resell it, but I can only offer the price I quoted."

I look at the items the women have spread on the table. Most pieces are costume jewelry, and I know Verity won't buy that for resale in her store.

The older woman is wearing skinny jeans and a leopard-print jacket. She has what Sly would call 'big hair,' and as I get closer, her heavy perfume about takes my breath away. She scoops the items from the table and stuffs them into a backpack.

"Wait." The younger woman speaks for the first time. "I have something you might be interested in." She reaches into the pocket of her baggy jeans and pulls out a necklace which she reverently lays in front of Verity.

We all press closer to take a look. A single gold bar is attached to a delicate gold chain. A topaz stone glitters near the bottom of the bar, and the initial S is engraved in the middle.

"That is lovely," Verity says. "But are you sure you want to sell such a personal piece?"

Leopard woman gasps, then turns it into a cough. "Honestly, Ro ... um ... S ... Susie," the woman stammers. "Put that away. There's no need for you to sell your favorite necklace." She plucks up the necklace and stuffs it into her backpack with the other jewelry. Then she grabs the younger woman by the arm and practically carries her toward the door.

"Susie," I call out, but both women keep moving. "Susie!"

Leopard woman stops and nudges 'Susie,' who turns and looks at me in confusion.

"Happy birthday," I say with what I hope looks like a genuine smile.

"What?" Her forehead scrunches in confusion.

"Happy birthday month," I explain.

Susie shakes her head and says, "My birthday is in July," even as Leopard woman drags her through the door and onto the sidewalk. The bell hasn't even stopped tinkling behind them before I'm out the door. I watch them hustle down the sidewalk, quickly climb into a dirty brown SUV, and race away.

I hurry back into the shop repeating a series of letters and numbers. Verity and Grace stare at me.

"Verity, do you have a pen and paper?" I ask breathlessly.

Without a word, Verity produces them, and I write down the information I memorized from the license plates. Then I take a deep breath and say, "I need to call Nick right now!"

"Jess, please tell me what's going on?" Verity asks. "Did you know those women?"

I shake my head. "No. But if that girl's name is Susie, then

I'm Taylor Swift. And when I wished her happy birthday month, she said her birthday is in July, which has a ruby for the birthstone. The stone in that necklace is a topaz, which is November."

I pull out my phone and speed dial Nick's number.

"And I've seen that necklace before," I say. "It belongs to Sierra."

Silence Can Be Deadly

Trouble in Pleasant Valley

Book Three

It started with a taxi ride ... or did it?

Forced from the career he loved and into driving a taxi, Peter Grace had grown accustomed to his simple life. Until one night when a suspicious fare and a traffic jam blew it all apart, and he was on the run again. Only this time it wasn't a matter of changing occupations but of life and death.

He needed help and he knew where to find it. His old friend Rafe in Pleasant Valley. What he didn't count on was finding not only the help he needed but a community of new friends and the love of his life. Zoe Poole.

The story of Captain Nate Zuberi and his wife Madison continues as they too risk their lives to help Peter. Along with Peter, Rafe, and Zoe, they strive to catch an assassin.

But can the group of friends find the killer before anyone else gets hurt?

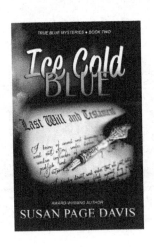

Ice Cold Blue
by Susan Page Davis

Book Two of the True Blue Mysteries Series

Campbell McBride is now working for her father Bill as a private investigator in Murray, Kentucky. Xina Harrison wants them to find out what is going on with her aunt, Katherine Taylor. Katherine is a rich, reclusive author, and she has resisted letting Xina visit her for several years. Xina arrived unannounced, and Katherine was upset and didn't want to let her in. When Xina did gain entry, she learned Katherine fired her longtime housekeeper. She noticed that a few family heirlooms previously on display have disappeared. Xina is afraid someone is stealing from her aunt or influencing her to give them her money and valuables. True Blue accepts the case, and the investigators follow a twisting path to the truth.

Scrivenings
PRESS
Quench your thirst for story.
www.ScriveningsPress.com

Stay up-to-date on your favorite books and authors with our free e-newsletters.

ScriveningsPress.com

Made in the USA
Monee, IL
05 December 2021

83383364R00111